S.CREAM SHOP

Revenge of the Gargoyle

D0017542

By Tracey West

Copyright © 2003 by Tracey West. Illustrations copyright © 2003 by Brian W. Dow. All rights reserved. Published by Grosset & Dunlap, a division of Penguin Young Readers Group, 345 Hudson Street, New York, New York 10014. Printed in the U.S.A.

Library of Congress Cataloging-in-Publication Data

West, Tracey, 1965–
  Revenge of the gargoyle / by Tracey West ; illustrated by Brian W. Dow.
    p. cm. — (Scream shop ; 4)
Summary: When a teenager selects a marble from Sebastian Cream's Junk Shop, she is unaware that it is the missing eye of one very angry gargoyle.
  ISBN 0-448-43227-7 (pbk.)
  [1. Gargoyles—Fiction. 2. Plot-your-own stories. 3. Horror stories.] I. Dow, Brian, ill. II. Title. III. Series.
  PZ7.W51937Re 2003
  [Fic]—dc22
                                        2003016065

ISBN 0-448-43227-7   A B C D E F G H I J

S.CREAM SHOP

Revenge of the Gargoyle

By Tracey West
Illustrated by Brian W. Dow

Grosset & Dunlap • New York

Tania Robbins was in a bad mood.

She'd pretty much been in a bad mood ever since Jennifer Delgado had moved into town last month. Before Jennifer, Tania had been one of the most popular sixth-grade girls at Ariana Bleaker Elementary School. She was the star of the girls' softball team. She pitched every game, and batted fourth in every lineup, the spot for the strongest hitter on the team.

But Jennifer Delgado was better at everything Tania did—at least, that's what everyone thought. Jennifer pitched the first half of every game. And Coach Merker let Jennifer bat fourth now. Tania batted third, which wasn't nearly as cool.

In yesterday's game against the team from August Bleaker Elementary School across town, Jennifer hit a game-winning home run. Nobody bothered to mention that Tania had hit a double right beforehand, knocking in two runs. No. All anyone talked about was Jennifer's home run.

That's why Tania had decided to walk home alone from school today. Usually, she walked home with her best friend Lincoln, but even he couldn't stop talking about Jennifer. Tania had just about all she could take.

Tania stomped along the streets of Bleaktown, staring at the cracks in the sidewalk as she walked. She took a different route than usual to avoid Lincoln.

By the time Tania actually looked up, she found that she was on an unfamiliar street. The sign read, "Wary Lane."

Tania scowled. "Great," she muttered. "Now I'm lost."

She decided she might as well walk down the street. She passed a few ordinary shops. Then one shop caught her eye.

The sign above the window read: "Sebastian Cream's Junk Shop." Tania crossed the street to get a closer look at the collection of unusual items in the window.

An antique record player sat on top of a wooden table with legs carved to look like lion's claws. A cement garden gnome with peeling paint stood at the foot of an old doll's carriage filled with china dolls. And on the floor in front of the window was an old cigar box filled with marbles.

Tania pressed her face to the window to get a closer look. Her grandfather collected marbles, and his birthday was just next week. A new marble would make a great present. She even had some money in her wallet.

Tania's bad mood lifted as she approached the door of the shop. It opened, and Evan Kim, a boy from her school, walked out. Tania said hi to Evan and stepped into the shop.

Shelves crowded with knickknacks seemed to fill almost every space in the shop. Tania made her way down the narrow aisle toward the elderly man at the counter. He looked up and smiled when he saw Tania.

"I'd like to look at the marbles in the window, please," Tania said.

The man walked to the window, taking small, quick steps, and returned with the cigar box.

"A lovely collection," he said. "Are you looking for something special?"

"A present for my grandfather," Tania replied. She began sorting through the marbles.

Tania had seen similar marbles in her grandfather's collection. Some were colored orange, blue, or red, with creamy swirls of white mixed in. Others were clear, with tiny flecks of color. All nice, but nothing really special.

Tania dug her hand farther into the box and pulled out a marble larger than all the others. It was a deep, brilliant black—the color of the night sky. It seemed to glow from somewhere within.

"This is the one," Tania said. Her grandfather didn't have anything like it.

The man nodded. "I had a feeling you'd pick that one," he said. He held out his hand. "Nice to meet you. I'm Sebastian Cream, the shop's proprietor."

"My name's Tania," she said, shaking his hand. "So, how much is the marble?"

Mr. Cream looked into Tania's eyes for a few seconds. Finally, he said, "Three dollars."

Tania couldn't believe her luck. She'd expected the marble to cost much more. She paid for the marble, and Mr. Cream packed it in a bag for her. Then she left the store.

By the time Tania got home and ate dinner, her bad mood had just about disappeared. Her mom had made hamburgers and macaroni and cheese, her favorite meal. So, when Lincoln knocked on the door, wanting to work on their science report, Tania didn't say no.

"How come you didn't wait for me after school today?" Lincoln asked, bounding up the stairs behind Tania.

"I had to get my grandfather a birthday present," Tania said. It wasn't exactly a lie, and she didn't feel like talking about Jennifer right now.

"It's Grandpa's birthday? Cool! What did you get?" Lincoln asked, flopping into Tania's desk chair.

Lincoln lived right down the street. He and

Tania had known each other ever since nursery school. Lincoln didn't have any grandparents, and he thought of Tania's grandfather as his own.

Tania picked her knapsack off of the floor, unzipped it, and took out the bag that Mr. Cream had given her. She carefully unwrapped the marble.

"Isn't it cool?" she said, holding it up to the light.

Just as before, the marble seemed to glow from within. Tania could make out her reflection in the marble's surface. But her dark hair looked all distorted in the marble's curves.

"Let me see," Lincoln said, taking the marble from her. He turned it over in his fingers, a serious expression on his round face. "It doesn't look like glass. I wonder what it's made of?"

He handed the marble back to Tania. "I took a geology book out of the library for our report," she said. "Maybe there's something in there."

Tania and Lincoln's report was about the rocks and minerals in their region. While they researched the report, they looked for rocks that looked like the marble. But they couldn't find any.

After an hour had passed, Tania's mother called up the stairs.

"Lincoln, it's getting late! Time to go home," she called.

"I bet Grandpa is going to really like the marble, no matter what it's made of," Lincoln said as he gathered his things.

"I know he is," Tania said confidently.

Tania and Lincoln headed downstairs.

"See you at school tomorrow," said Tania, as she walked Lincoln to the door.

"Okay," said Lincoln. "Good night."

Tania walked back up to her bedroom. She sat down on her bed and grabbed the marble. She examined it again, and held it under the light of her bedroom lamp.

Suddenly, a dark shadow blocked out the light. Startled, Tania looked up.

A huge creature crouched on the roof of her window, peering into her room through the open window. It looked like some kind of monster— with smooth, gray skin, claws, and a craggy face with one glittering, black eye.

Tania froze, paralyzed with fear. From somewhere deep in her mind, a single word emerged:

Gargoyle.

This thing was a gargoyle. One of those statues perched on top of old buildings and churches.

But this one was perched outside her window.

And he was alive.

Then the gargoyle spoke.

"Give me back my eye!" the gargoyle demanded

in a gruff, growling voice. His single eye was fixed on the black marble in Tania's hand.

Tania gulped nervously, and slowly stood up.

If Tania gives the marble to the gargoyle, go to page 12.

If Tania runs out of the room, go to page 17.

If Tania tries to talk to the gargoyle, go to page 23.

Continued from page 11

The gargoyle wanted the marble. Her grandfather's present.

But Tania was too terrified to argue. She quickly tossed the black marble to the gargoyle. He caught it in his claw. Then he carefully inserted the marble into his empty eye socket.

What have I done? Tania's mind raced. *He's probably going to try to eat me or something. I should have run when I had the chance.* She began to slowly back up toward her bedroom door.

Then, amazingly, the gargoyle smiled. At least, it looked like a smile.

"Thank you," the gargoyle said. "I am Kragg. It has been difficult for me since I lost my eye. I am sorry to trouble you." The creature turned his huge body around and started to climb back out the window.

"Wait!" Tania cried, finally finding her voice. The gargoyle's friendly manner had eased her fears. Her curiosity took over. "Who are you? I mean, what are you? I mean—"

The gargoyle looked back at Tania. "I am sorry. I am grateful for your help," he said. "But I am on a mission to save my people. Without a willing human to help us, all will be lost. I must hurry before it's too late."

Mission? Willing human? Now Tania was more curious than ever. Without thinking, she blurted out, "What kind of willing human? Maybe I can help you."

The gargoyle paused. He looked thoughtful for a minute. Then he shook his head. "It is too dangerous for a mere girl. I cannot risk it."

"*Mere* girl!" Tania bristled at the words. "Who do you think you're talking to? I'm good enough to help you with your problem. But you obviously don't want my help."

The gargoyle nodded. "You are right. I learned long ago to judge others by their spirit, not by their appearance. Let me tell you of my mission. If you would still like to help, I will gladly accept it."

For a split second, Tania felt like she must be crazy. Here she was, in her room with a giant, living gargoyle. But instead of running and screaming and calling the police, she was offering to help him with some kind of mission. It felt like some kind of wacky dream.

"Uh, you can sit down if you want," Tania said awkwardly. She tossed her sweatshirt off of her desk chair, then realized how foolish that must have seemed. The gargoyle was three times as wide as the chair—and probably ten times as heavy.

The gargoyle climbed down from the windowsill and crouched on the floor. A shaft of moonlight shone through the window, making his marble eyes glitter. Tania felt goose bumps pop up on her arms. She still couldn't believe this was happening.

"Let me begin," he said. "As I said, I am Kragg."

"And I'm Tania," Tania added. She sat on the edge of her bed.

Kragg nodded. "Long ago, a foul darkness threatened the Earth," he began. "A darkness as old as the beginning of time. To fight the darkness, a guild of stone carvers created me and my kind."

"You mean gargoyles?" Tania asked.

"Some call us that," Kragg said. "True gargoyles were used as waterspouts on buildings. Those of us who are statues are known as grotesques."

Tania made a face. "You don't look grotesque to me. You look pretty cool. But I like the name gargoyle better."

"What we are called is not important," Kragg said, "but our mission is. During the day, we are as still as stone, unable to move. But the stonecutters went to the alchemists for help. They used their magical talents to create a life force. That life force allows us to awaken each night. We patrol the Earth, keeping the Dark One at bay."

"Wow," Tania said. "How come nobody knows about this?"

"It is not necessary," Kragg replied. "We protect humans from the darkness. It has been that way for centuries. We do not require thanks for our actions. Our mission is our reward."

"So why do you need a human to help you now?" Tania asked.

Kragg's expression darkened. "We have kept the darkness at bay for centuries. Long ago, its power faded. It feared our strength. But the Dark One has new strength now. And it plans to destroy us."

Anger and desperation tinged Kragg's voice.

"The life force that sustains us is kept in a chalice," the gargoyle continued. "The alchemists hid the chalice in an underground chamber. They cast a spell over the chamber so that nothing inhuman could enter it. That spell has kept the life force safe for a very long time. But there have been stirrings . . . we fear that the Dark One may have found a way of getting to the life force. If that happens, we will remain stone forever, unable to fulfill our mission. Evil will overcome the Earth."

Tania shivered. But Kragg hadn't fully answered her question. "So you need a human to enter the chamber for you? Why?" she asked.

"We want to get the life force before the Dark One finds it," Kragg said. "We want to remove it from the chamber and protect it ourselves. We were hoping to find an alchemist . . ."

"I could look in the Yellow Pages, but I don't think you'll have much luck," Tania said.

"That is our mission, Tania," Kragg said. "Will you help us?"

Tania hesitated. All this stuff about dark forces made her wonder if she had spoken up too soon. Sure, she could play softball—but could she fight evil?

If Tania agrees to help the gargoyles, go to page 32.

If Tania plays it safe and tells Kragg she can't help him, go to page 65.

Instinct took over. Tania raced out of her bedroom, down the stairs, through the front door, and into the night. She ran like she had hit one deep into left field and was trying to get to home. She ran down the street, still clutching the marble in her hand. She wasn't sure where she was going—just sure that she wanted to get away from that gargoyle as fast as she could.

She bumped into Lincoln without even realizing it.

"Hey, what's the rush?" Lincoln asked. "Is your house on fire or something?"

"It's the marble," Tania said, still running as Lincoln struggled to catch up. "This gargoyle came into my room, and—"

She couldn't explain it. But she knew someone who might be able to. Tania sped off toward her grandfather's house.

"Hey, wait for me!" Lincoln called.

Tania's grandfather lived just a few blocks away, in a small red brick house on the corner of Maple and Green. She bounded up the steps and started banging the door knocker—Grandpa Martin didn't like doorbells. She almost fell backwards off the step when she noticed the shape of the door knocker for the first time.

It looked like the head of a gargoyle.

Just then, Grandpa Martin opened the door.

"Hey there, Muffin," he said. "What are you doing out so late?"

"Something weird happened, Grandpa," Tania said. "I need to talk to you about it."

"Something weird?" he asked, letting Tania inside.

"Something about a gargoyle," Lincoln said, puffing and panting. He climbed the stairs and followed Tania into the house. "Hey, Grandpa."

"Nice to see you, Lincoln," Grandpa Martin replied.

Grandpa Martin led them into his living room. He plopped down on his favorite armchair, while Tania and Lincoln sat on the soft, brown couch.

Just being in the room made Tania feel calmer. Grandpa had taught history before he retired, and bookshelves lined every wall of the house. Every book stood perfectly straight on its shelf. The neatness and order made the whole gargoyle episode seem pretty silly. But if anyone would believe her, Grandpa would.

"Now what on earth is the matter?" Grandpa asked.

Tania took a deep breath. She opened her hand to reveal the black marble.

"I got this for you for your birthday, from

some weird shop downtown," Tania said. "I showed it to Lincoln, but then he had to go home."

"She's right so far," Lincoln said, trying to be helpful.

"I was in my room," Tania said. "And something came up to my window. I think it was a gargoyle. It had wings, and it was gray, and it had this monster face, and—"

"Hold on there now," Grandpa said. "Are you sure it was a gargoyle? It must have been an owl or some other kind of bird."

Tania shook her head. "It wasn't an owl. It was a gargoyle. And then it talked to me. It looked at the marble and said, 'Give me back my eye!' And then I ran."

Grandpa looked deep in thought. Then he took the marble from Tania's hands.

"Maybe it was a gargoyle you saw, and maybe it wasn't," he said. "But this is definitely an unusual stone. If we learn more about the marble, we may be able to figure out what happened to you."

Tania let out a breath. She knew Grandpa Martin wouldn't think she was being silly, or making up stories.

Grandpa took his eyeglasses from the pocket of his faded flannel shirt and walked over to one of the many bookcases in the room.

"Let's see now," he said, muttering to himself. Finally, with an "Aha!" he stood on his toes and grabbed a book from the top shelf.

"It's just a hunch," Grandpa said. "This might just be an ordinary marble. But I think I've seen something like it before."

Grandpa sat down in his chair and opened the book. Tania leaned closer to read the title: *A History of Legendary Stones.*

Grandpa Martin flipped through the pages for a few minutes while Lincoln asked Tania countless questions about the gargoyle. What did he look like? What did he smell like? Where did he come from? Tania mostly ignored Lincoln and tapped her foot impatiently on the wood floor. She wanted answers—now.

"Hmm." Grandpa Martin set the book on his lap. "Just as I thought. It's that inner glow that gives it away. I've never seen anything like it."

"What did you find?" Tania asked. She got up and knelt on the floor next to Grandpa's chair. Lincoln did the same.

"This marble is part of a set of four called the Stones of Power," Grandpa explained. "Besides the black marble, there is a gold one, a silver one, and a white one."

"What kind of power do they have?" Lincoln asked.

"Read for yourself," Grandpa said.

The story is pretty interesting, Tania thought. As Tania and Lincoln read, they learned that the stones used to be kept in a museum in Italy. When kept together, they possessed amazing powers. Then a stone carver stole them and brought them to America. He carved four gargoyle statues and used the stones for eyes. Then he placed the gargoyles around his town . . .

"Bleaktown!" Tania and Lincoln said excitedly.

According to the book, the gargoyles had the power to come to life at night. The stones gave them an extra power—to fight off evil. There was even a rhyme about where the gargoyles could be found:

Where white is found, men go to pray.
The black is found where night meets day.
Find the silver in the round.
Find the gold where knowledge is found.

"Hey, I bet I know where the white marble is," Tania said. "There are lots of weird carvings on top of our church. One of them might be a gargoyle."

"I figured out the silver one," Lincoln said. "There's a park shaped like a circle on the edge of town. My aunt lives near there. The gargoyle must be there!"

Grandpa Martin laughed. "This is a book of legends, remember? Not facts."

"It can't hurt to look, can it?" Tania asked.

"I'm with you," Lincoln said. "But which one should we look for first?"

If Tania and Lincoln search for the white marble first, go to page 76.

If Tania and Lincoln search for the silver marble first, go to page 91.

Continued from page 11

"D-D-Do you mean this marble?" Tania asked, her voice shaking.

"That is my eye," the gargoyle growled. "Return it to me at once!"

"B-But I bought it for my grandfather," she stuttered. "It's his birthday present!"

The gargoyle's lone black eye flashed. "Return it now!"

His tone of voice told her that talking wasn't the best way to go. She held out the marble in her shaking hand . . . and then dropped it. The marble landed on the floor.

"Sorry!" Tania said quickly, bending down to get it.

Then she stopped. The gargoyle had stopped moving completely. Tania straightened up.

"Hello?" she asked. "Mr. Gargoyle?" She waved her hand in front of his face.

That's odd, Tania thought. Then she noticed that her room seemed strangely quiet. The hands on her bedside clock had stopped moving. Sunny, the goldfish she kept in a bowl on her dresser, had frozen in his bowl in mid-swim.

It must be the marble, Tania realized. *It has the power to freeze stuff*.

Tania looked at the marble, then at the gargoyle. A marble that could freeze stuff could come in pretty handy. She wouldn't mind keeping it for a while. Besides, she didn't know for sure that it really belonged to the gargoyle. She'd paid for it fair and square, right?

Tania wasn't sure how long the freezing would last. She quickly scooped up the marble and charged down the stairs, yelling something to her mother about Lincoln forgetting his science book. She didn't stop running until she reached Lincoln's house.

"Tania, what's wrong?" Lincoln asked, shutting the door behind her.

"I've got to tell you something," she said. "Alone."

That wasn't easy in Lincoln's house. He had two older brothers and two younger brothers, and none of them had their own room. Luckily, the two brothers Lincoln shared a room with were out at the movies, so Tania and Lincoln went into the older boys' room and closed the door.

"Something happened after you left," Tania said. Then she launched into her story.

"And you brought the marble *here*?" Lincoln asked when she was finished. He looked panicked. "Are you bonkers? That gargoyle is probably following you right now. You should give it back to him."

"He was still frozen when I left," Tania pointed out. "Besides, I ran fast. He doesn't know where I am."

Lincoln shook his head. "What are you going to do with it, anyway?"

Tania's eyes shone. "Just think about it, Linc," she said. "Imagine if you could freeze time around you. If you're late for school, you could use the marble to take your shower and eat your breakfast. If you can't finish a test, you could use the marble to give yourself more time . . ."

"I don't know," Lincoln said. "This is too weird. I really think you should give back the marble."

If Tania decides to give the marble back to the gargoyle, go to page 52.

If Tania decides to keep the marble and try it out, go to page 112.

Continued from page 46

Don't listen to it, Tania told herself. *It's a trick. You need to help Kragg.*

But she could feel the Dark One pulling at her—almost like it had curled up inside her brain like a snake. And she liked what she heard.

"Tania! Are you all right?" Kragg called out.

Tania wanted to answer, but she couldn't. Visions danced in her mind—hitting home run after home run at every game, winning the state championship for her team, crowds of people cheering her name . . .

"What do I need to do?" Tania whispered.

The Dark One laughed. "Very good, Tania," he said. "Very good indeed. It's simple. All you need to do is drink from the chalice. Drink the life force of the gargoyles. Drink in all of their power and strength."

Then Tania heard Kragg's voice, but it seemed far, far away.

"Tania, who are you talking to? If someone is in the chamber with you, then you must leave—quickly."

But the Dark One had complete power over Tania now. She lifted the chalice off the pedestal and raised it to her mouth. A sweet, clean smell filled her nostrils. Inside the silver cup, the life force of the gargoyles shimmered and sparkled, like a night sky full of fireflies.

In the back of her mind, Tania heard Kragg cry out in agony.

He must be trying to enter the chamber, she thought. *But he can't. I'm in control here.*

"Tania, you must not drink the life force!" Kragg yelled.

Tania could not ignore Kragg any longer. He was an annoyance that must be stopped.

"You only want it for yourself!" she shouted. A small part of her wondered where the words came from. "Well, it's mine now!"

"The Dark One will have complete power over you once you drink the life force," Kragg cried out. "If you drink it, he will use you to carry out his evil plans!"

"He's lying," whispered the Dark One. "Drink it. Drink it now."

Tania lifted the cup to her lips. But, before she could drink, something slammed into the chalice, sending it flying from her hands.

"No!" Tania cried.

A rock had hit the chalice. It clattered to the floor, sending the life force spilling over the pillar.

"Fool!" came the voice of the Dark One. "You have sealed your doom!"

Tania looked at the fallen chalice, horrified.

What had she done? She ran to the chamber door.

"I had to do it, Tania," Kragg said, but each word came out more slowly than the last. "I had to keep . . . our . . . power . . . away . . . from . . . it."

Kragg's movements slowed until they came to a complete stop. The light in his black marble eyes slowly faded.

He stood at the chamber door, as still as a statue.

"No!" Tania shrieked. She spun around, searching for some sign of the evil force that had caused all of this. "What have you done?" she called out to the Dark One.

The low voice of the Dark One hissed in her ear.

"It is not what *I* have done, Tania," it whispered. "But what you have done."

Tania knew it was all her fault. *She* had listened to the Dark One. And *she* had spilled the life force. Now it was all over. Kragg had turned to stone. And it was all her fault.

THE END

Continued from page 48

"Tell me more," Tania said.

Talbot grinned and held out his hand. "I can do better than tell you," he said. "I can *show* you. Touch my hand."

"Tania, no!" Lincoln shouted.

But Tania ignored him. Power . . . fame . . . glory . . . . It couldn't hurt to find out more. She held out her hand.

At first, Talbot's ghostly hand felt cold and clammy, like fog. But then an electric jolt shot from his fingertips, coursing through her own. The next second, her brain was crowded with images.

She saw Talbot—solid and human—stealing the marbles. It was like watching scenes from a movie at super-fast speed. She saw him in a dark, windowless room, watching the marbles as they swirled in front of him. She heard him speaking to the marbles in a strange language—a language that she suddenly understood. She saw him outside now, on a dark night, stopping a plump man in a long coat. Talbot whispered to the marbles, and beams of light shot from them, transforming the man into a hideous stone gargoyle. She watched as the power of the marbles lifted Talbot into the air, sending him soaring into the night sky.

Talbot removed his hand. Tania gasped.

She understood now. She knew what the marbles could do—and exactly how to use them.

And she couldn't wait.

Tania held out her palm and began speaking to the marbles in the strange language she had absorbed through Talbot. The marbles stopped swirling, hovered in position for a second, and then smoothly glided over and landed in Tania's palm.

"Excellent!" Talbot said. "You make a fine student. Tell me, what would you like to do first?"

Tania stared at the glowing marbles in her palm. She could feel their energy coursing through her, and she liked it. She remembered the vision of Talbot turning the man into stone, and grinned.

"I can think of someone I'd like to use these on," she said. "Jennifer Delgado won't be able to hit any home runs if she's a statue!"

Lincoln stepped between Tania and Talbot, a look of panic on his face.

"Tania, are you crazy?" he asked. "You don't want to hurt Jennifer. You don't want to hurt anybody! This isn't like you."

Tania shook her head. "Silly Lincoln. You don't have the power. You don't understand."

Lincoln ran away and hopped on his bike. "I'll

stop you! I'll tell Grandpa Martin! I'll warn Jennifer! I won't let you hurt anyone!"

Tania's face clouded. She began whispering to the marbles again.

They bounced in her hand like popcorn kernels over a flame. Then beams of white, black, silver, and gold light shot from them, zapping Lincoln.

"No!" Lincoln screamed, but it was too late. Tania watched as Lincoln's body twisted into the shape of a crouching, stone gargoyle.

"Nicely done," said Talbot.

"I agree," Tania said, her eyes gleaming. "And now it's Jennifer's turn!"

THE END

Tania took a deep breath. Whoever helped Kragg and the gargoyles would be a real hero. How often did you get a chance to do that?

"I'll help you," she said. Then she had an idea. "Can my friend Lincoln help, too?"

"Can he be trusted?" the gargoyle asked.

"Well, he did stick up for Jennifer Delgado the other day," Tania said. That still hurt. "But he's not a bad guy. I'm sure we can trust him."

Kragg nodded. "Fine. Tomorrow night, we can meet on the outskirts of the hidden chamber."

Kragg gave Tania directions to the chamber, which was hidden in a mountain on the edge of Bleaktown. Tania was surprised. From the sound of Kragg's story, she had expected the chamber to be in some exotic, foreign place.

"Be there when the sun goes down," Kragg said. Then he vanished into the darkness.

The next day, after dinner, Tania and Lincoln rode their bikes through Bleaktown.

"I still can't believe you talked me into this," Lincoln complained. "You tell me a gargoyle climbed into your window last night. He wants you to meet him in some cavern somewhere so you can save the world. Are you sure you weren't dreaming?"

"I know it sounds crazy, but it's real," Tania said. "You'll see for yourself, soon."

Lincoln shook his head, but he kept pedaling. A few minutes later, they reached the foot of the mountain.

"What now?" Lincoln asked.

"Kragg said there'd be a trail," Tania said. Both sides of the road were surrounded by woods. Tania scanned the landscape until she noticed a break between the trees on the right. "There it is!" she cried.

The trail looked narrow and bumpy, so Tania and Lincoln left their bikes behind. Above them, the sun streaked the sky red as they made their way through the trees.

The trail hugged the side of the mountain. To the left, they could see its craggy surface. Weeds and flowers grew through cracks in the rocks. Tania kept her eyes on the mountainside, searching for the cavern.

"Are you sure this is the right way?" Lincoln asked after they had walked for fifteen minutes. "It's going to be dark soon."

Just as Lincoln finished his sentence, Tania spotted the cavern.

"We're here," she said.

"Okay," Lincoln said. "So where's this gargoyle?"

At that moment, the last rays of the sun disappeared behind the horizon. Tania took a flash-light out of her backpack. It barely lit up the pitch-black cavern. Kragg had said he would meet her here. Should they go inside?

Suddenly, a strange cry echoed through the forest. Tania and Lincoln looked up. There, against the light of the full moon, four birds flew in a circle.

The birds circled downward, and Tania real-ized with excitement that they weren't birds at all.

They were gargoyles!

One by one, the gargoyles landed at the mouth of the cavern. Tania watched breathlessly as the first three gargoyles silently marched into the cavern. Kragg, the final gargoyle, stopped in front of Tania.

"See, Lincoln?" Tania said. "I told you I was telling the truth."

But Lincoln didn't answer. Tania turned to her friend to see him frozen like a statue. He was clearly in shock.

Kragg looked at Lincoln. "Thank you for help-ing us," he said. "We should enter the cavern now. It is not safe out here."

"Uh . . . yeah," Lincoln muttered weakly. Tania practically had to drag him inside the cavern.

The gargoyles had started a small fire in the cavern and circled around it. Tania watched, fascinated, as the firelight danced across their gray faces. One had a round nose, a wide mouth, and large, pointy ears—like a bat's. Another had dog-like ears, but his snout was shaped like a large beak. Another one, smaller than the rest, had a squished-up face and small round ears.

The beak-faced gargoyle snorted. "*These* are the humans who will save us, Kragg? You have put our future in the hands of *children*?"

"The Dark One grows closer, Elias," Kragg replied. "These humans have agreed to help us. They may be our only hope."

Elias snorted again, but he did not challenge Kragg. He opened his clawed hand to reveal an ancient scroll of paper.

"Well, I did not fail in my quest," Elias said. "I have found the map. It should lead us to the chamber."

"And I have not failed either," said the gargoyle with the squished-up face. "I found the rhyme that reveals the location of the chamber."

The gargoyle recited the rhyme in a singsong voice:

"Where the snake turns, there turn I.
To the water's edge I fly.
Then travel to where the secrets lie."

The gargoyles murmured their approval.

"We should split up," Kragg suggested. "Some

can follow the map. Others can follow the rhyme. With luck, we'll find the chamber before morning dawns."

Suddenly, a loud rumbling sound filled the chamber. Tania felt a cold chill sweep through her body. The fire blew out in a single gust.

Then the ceiling began to cave in.

Before Tania could react, she felt Kragg's strong arm grab her. He pulled her deeper into the cavern. Panicked, Tania looked around for Lincoln and saw Elias dragging him outside, through the mouth of the cave.

To follow Tania and Kragg, go to page 59.

To follow Lincoln and Elias, go to page 79.

Continued from page 70

Tania knew Lincoln was right. She didn't want to skip practice.

"Tomorrow morning," Tania agreed. "Let's leave early."

Lincoln nodded. Tania had to make up a story about extra softball practice to get out of Sunday family brunch, but she still made it to Lincoln's doorstep at nine o'clock sharp. Lincoln looked more excited than he had the day before.

"My mom gave me directions to my aunt's house," Lincoln said. "That's where the park is. And there's a gargoyle right in the middle of the park . . . I know exactly where to go."

Tania pulled a piece of paper from her jeans pocket. "And I went to Grandpa's last night and wrote down the rhyme. Once we find the silver marble, we'll need it to figure out where the gold one is."

Lincoln nodded and hopped on his bike. Tania followed him past the small, square houses of his neighborhood, down Main Street—which was deserted so early on a Sunday morning, and into a neighborhood she had never seen before. Large, fancy houses lined the streets.

They turned a corner and found themselves facing a large, round park, surrounded by an ivy-covered stone wall. *It is much nicer than Bleaktown Park*, Tania decided when they pedaled inside. Red and purple flowers grew around marble benches. Old-fashioned street lamps flanked the benches. A stream ran around the entire circle, passable by a covered bridge.

And in the very center, atop a tall pedestal, sat a gargoyle.

Excited, Tania hopped off her bike, let it fall in the grass, and ran to the pedestal. This gargoyle sat on all fours, like a cat, but crouched forward. It had short, stubby ears, a square nose, and a stone tongue sticking out of its mouth.

But Tania was most interested in its eyes—two shiny, silver marbles.

"We found it!" she cheered. "Lincoln, you are amazing!"

Tania climbed up the pedestal, which turned out to be much easier to do than climbing up the stone wall of the church. Just like before, the two eyes looked the same, except one—the left one, this time—had a distinct inner glow. Tania used her penknife to pop out the eye, being careful to catch it this time. Then she climbed back down.

"Let's see what happens this time," Tania said. She and Lincoln sat down on one of the benches. Tania took the black marble out of her pocket first and placed it on the bench between them. She placed the white marble a few inches away, and did the same with the silver marble, to form a triangle.

The marbles glowed brightly and began to roll toward one another.

And then something amazing happened.

The marbles gently floated into the air and began to swirl around in a kind of dance. Tania gasped.

"That is so cool!" Lincoln exclaimed.

"Imagine what will happen when we find the gold one," Tania said. Leaving the marbles to their dance, she took out the rhyme from her pocket.

"Find the gold where knowledge is found," Tania read.

She thought quietly for a moment.

"That could be so many places," Tania finally said. "Where should we look first?"

"How about the library?" Lincoln suggested.

Tania frowned. "I don't know. I've been to the library lots of times, but I've never seen a gargoyle there."

"You didn't know there was a gargoyle at the church, either," Lincoln pointed out.

"That's true," Tania admitted. Then Tania

exclaimed, "Hey! What about Bleaktown College?"

"That's a great idea," Lincoln agreed. "Which place should we check out first?"

If Tania and Lincoln go to Bleaktown College, go to page 49.

If Tania and Lincoln go to the library, go to page 127.

Continued from page 82

Lincoln looked behind him. The birds had changed direction. Instead of heading toward Elias, they were speeding right toward him.

Suddenly, Elias took flight. He flew faster than the birds. He and Lincoln reached the hole at the same time. Lincoln felt Elias's strong arms push him inside the hole.

Lincoln landed with a thud on the hard ground below. Elias swooped down, folded his wings, and glided to a stop.

"You humans are good for nothing," Elias said. "I was using a chant that would have transformed the birds back into their original form. But when they followed you, the power of the chant ended."

Lincoln felt terrible. He had wanted to prove that he could be helpful, and he had just made things worse. Outside, above the hole, the birds screeched and flapped their wings.

"Can they get in?" Lincoln asked worriedly.

"They won't need to," Elias said. "The Dark One has us where he wants us."

Elias had barely finished the sentence when Lincoln heard a loud, scraping noise above them. He looked up to see a large boulder being dragged over the hole.

Then everything went pitch-black.

"We are trapped," Elias said bitterly. "We cannot find the chalice now."

Lincoln was frightened. *What were they going to do now?* He tried desperately to think of a way out—some way to make it up to Elias. Lincoln tried screaming. He tried banging on the hole. But no one came to their rescue.

Just when he was about to give up all hope, Lincoln finally heard the boulder being pushed aside. Tania and Kragg looked down into the hole.

"We did it!" Tania said, shining her flashlight into the hole. "We got the chalice and defeated the Dark One. Then we started our search for you. Kragg heard your voice and we found you here. Are you okay?"

"At least the girl is good for something," Elias muttered. "She got the chalice. But this one here," he pointed at Lincoln in disgust, "he's another story."

Lincoln felt like staying in the hole. He couldn't face Tania and Kragg after what had happened.

"Oh, well," Lincoln said, looking on the bright side. "At least I didn't get killed by a bunch of birds!"

THE END

Continued from page 85

"What do you think, Kragg?" Tania asked.

Kragg thought for a minute. Finally, he said, "The chamber is supposed to be hidden deep in the mountain. Perhaps we should follow the water downstream. It will lead us farther underground."

Tania looked at the water. It wasn't exactly a bubbling stream, but she could see the water slowly rippling toward the right.

"Sounds good to me," Tania said. "Let's give it a try."

Tania shone the flashlight down the path. They walked in silence for a few minutes. Soon, the path began to grow narrower. Kragg's head brushed the roof of the cave, and there wasn't much extra space between the edge of the stream and the wall of the passage. They had to walk in a single file, with Tania leading the way. Tania felt a new chill in the air and shivered.

"I'll be glad when we're out in the open again," Tania remarked. "You must be feeling worse than I am. You're so much bigger than us."

"You forget who I am," Kragg said. "I am a creature of stone. A creature of the dark."

"So I guess this is just your style, then, right?" Tania said.

"I suppose it is," Kragg replied.

As they walked on, Tania thought about what it must be like to be Kragg. Sure, sitting around all day frozen like a statue must be a drag. But then at night—to be able to fly, to be strong, so strong that nobody could stop you. That would be cool.

Then the flashlight beam illuminated something up ahead, and Tania snapped out of her daydream. The path had ended—and they had reached a door.

"I think we found it," Tania whispered. She shone the flashlight on the door's surface. Strange carvings and markings covered the stone.

"What do they mean?" Tania asked.

"It is an ancient language," Kragg said. "But I know some of it. The words warn against anything non-human entering the chamber."

"Where's the handle?" Tania asked.

The end of the path had widened enough so that Kragg and Tania could stand side by side. He stepped up next to her and examined the door. Soon, he pointed to an impression right in the center. It appeared to be a human hand.

"Perhaps that is the way," Kragg said.

Tania understood immediately. She opened her palm and reached out toward the door. Then she hesitated.

"So what am I supposed to do in there, exactly?" she asked.

"Find the chalice," Kragg said. "And then bring it to me."

Tania nodded. "Sounds easy enough." Then she turned toward the door and pressed her palm into the imprint in the stone.

The huge stone door slid to the side with a loud groan. Beyond the door, Tania could only see darkness. She took a deep breath. Maybe this wasn't going to be as easy as it sounded.

"You're not going anywhere, are you?" she asked Kragg.

The gargoyle shook his head. "I will be here if you need me."

That made Tania feel more confident. She held up her flashlight and stepped into the chamber.

She hadn't gone far when she spotted something up ahead, shining in the darkness. There, atop a stone pillar, rested a silver cup.

She had found the chalice.

"I see it!" Tania called out to Kragg. She stepped forward and reached out to grab the chalice when a cold chill swept over her. She stopped.

Then a low, hissing voice filled her head.

"Claim the chalice for yourself, Tania," said the voice. "Think of all the strength and power it will bring you."

Tania knew, without knowing how, exactly who

the voice belonged to. It was the Dark One. It had to be. If evil had a sound, that voice would be it.

Tania turned in a circle, aiming her flashlight in every corner of the chamber. No one was there.

"I thought you couldn't come into the chamber," Tania said nervously.

"I am not in the chamber," hissed the voice. "I am in your heart, Tania. I am inside the heart of every man, woman, and child on the planet, waiting to be set free. And you can help me."

"No way," Tania said. "I'm not stupid."

"Yes, you are," said the Dark One. "Stupid to turn down what I am offering you. Think about it, Tania. Strength and power. All that you want."

Enough strength and power to take back my place on the softball team, Tania thought, then immediately felt foolish.

"You're trying to trick me," she said.

"No, Tania," said the Dark One. "I am trying to help you."

If Tania is tempted by the Dark One, go to page 26.

If Tania continues to help Kragg and the gargoyles, go to page 132.

Continued from page 131

"These marbles are dangerous, Tania," Lincoln said. "Come on. You know I'm right."

"All right," she said. "I'll grab the marbles. You distract him."

"Distract him? How?" Lincoln asked, but Tania had already turned back to Talbot.

"We would love to help you," she said, smiling sweetly. "In fact, Sorcerer Lincoln over here will tell you all about our plans."

"Uh, that's right," Lincoln said, taking Tania's cue. "We're very evil, Tania and I. Very, very, evil. We've been looking for someone more evil than us for ages. That's why we went searching for those marbles . . ."

With Talbot's attention focused on Lincoln, Tania made her move. She quickly ran around Talbot, scooping up marbles as she went. When she had all four marbles, she raised them in the air.

"Wait!" Talbot cried. "Don't be foolish! Those marbles hold great power."

"It doesn't matter," Tania shot back. "Lincoln and I aren't evil. We're not going to help you get revenge on anybody. So say good-bye to your marbles."

"Wait!" Talbot cried again.

"What is it now?" Tania asked.

"Forget about your friend for a minute," Talbot said, smiling slyly. "And listen to me. I can teach you how to use the power of the marbles to obtain anything you want. Fame. Glory. Power."

Tania listened. Those things didn't sound evil. They sounded pretty cool.

"They can all be yours," Talbot said. "All you have to do is listen to me."

Tania thought quietly.

"Don't do it, Tania!" Lincoln cried.

If Tania accepts Talbot's offer, go to page 29.

If Tania refuses Talbot's offer, go to page 100.

Continued from page 40

"I think we should go to Bleaktown College," Tania decided. "I think the marble is there."

"Okay," said Lincoln. "Let's go."

But searching the college grounds was more than they bargained for. It took an hour to bike there, and they found the campus filled with stone, ivy-covered buildings. There could be a gargoyle lurking on any one of them, so they carefully searched each one.

Before they knew it, the sun was setting and their stomachs were growling.

"I guess you were right," Tania finally admitted. "We'll check out the library tomorrow."

Tania and Lincoln wearily pedaled their bikes down the long, tree-lined road that led out of the college. It was deserted, and the trees cast spooky-looking shadows on the pavement.

They were about halfway down the driveway when, suddenly, three figures emerged from the trees, blocking their path. Tania slammed on the brakes. Lincoln tried to, but went toppling off his bike.

Three angry-looking gargoyles stood before them. One had one black eye; the other had one white eye; and the other had one silver eye.

"Give us back our eyes!" growled the

gargoyle with the lone black eye.

This time, Tania didn't hesitate. She took all three marbles out of her pocket and tossed them at the gargoyles. Amazingly, the marbles gracefully flew through the air, each landing in the eye socket Tania had ripped it from.

"S-S-Sorry about all this," Tania stammered. "Well, I guess we'll be going now."

But the gargoyle shook his head.

"We have our eyes," he said, "But now we want our revenge!"

Tania heard Lincoln whimpering behind her. The gargoyles were circling them now. She could try to run, but the gargoyles had wings . . .

"IMMOBULUS!"

Tania couldn't believe it. Grandpa Martin's voice rang through the night air. At the sound of the words, the gargoyles froze in position. Grandpa pushed through them and motioned to Tania and Lincoln.

"Come on," he said. "This only lasts for a little while."

They quickly jogged alongside Grandpa Martin, pushing their bikes.

"Grandpa, what did you do?" Tania asked.

"I've been doing some research these last few days," he said, "and it looks like the whole story is true. I figured you two might be in trouble, so I looked for some kind of magical way to stop the gargoyles. I think they'll leave you alone now."

"Thanks, Grandpa," Tania said, looking over her shoulder at the three frozen forms of the gargoyles. "I sure hope so!"

THE END

Tania sighed. Lincoln made a lot of sense. Messing around with a magic marble wasn't exactly the smartest idea—especially when an angry gargoyle wanted it back.

"You're right, Lincoln," Tania said. "I'd better see if the gargoyle's still there."

As Tania jogged back down the street, she wasn't sure what she would find at home. Would the gargoyle still be frozen, like a statue, along with her goldfish? The thought that her mother may have gone up to her room while she was gone made her run a little faster. She entered her house and sped up the stairs.

But the gargoyle was not there, and her clock and Sunny the goldfish were back to normal. She sat on her bed, dazed. Had she just imagined everything?

To be safe, she carefully placed the marble on the window ledge and left her window open before she went to sleep. A few hours later, a clattering sound woke her from her dreams. Tania realized that the sound came from the window.

Could it be the gargoyle? Tania slowly opened one eye, her heart pounding.

There was no gargoyle by her window, only the curtains flapping slightly in the breeze. Tania noticed that something appeared to be glowing on the windowsill, but it didn't look like the black marble.

Tania turned on the light next to her bed and walked to the window. In place of the black marble glittered a pretty yellow one with orange streaks. Tania carefully picked it up. It wasn't quite as mysterious-looking as the black one, but it was still pretty cool.

Tania got up to check on Sunny. The goldfish still swam in circles around his bowl.

She rolled the marble along the floor. Yup—this was just a plain, ordinary marble.

Tania grinned. She still had a birthday present for her grandfather—and a pretty cool story to tell him, too.

THE END

Continued from page 107

Tania's gut told her she would be safer cutting through backyards than running out in the open. She tore across the nearest backyard she could find that didn't have a fence. She ran to the next house, jumping over a low row of bushes that bordered the yard.

She tried not to look back, but she clearly heard the sound of the gargoyle behind her, crashing through the bushes. She briefly wondered why he wasn't using his leathery wings to fly.

It might be the trees, she thought. Too much for him to fly through. Cutting through the yards was probably a good idea.

Then she heard a loud crash behind her, and turned around in spite of herself. In his hurry, the gargoyle had crashed into a plastic kiddie jungle gym. His wings were tangled in the chains of the swing. He grunted and struggled to get out.

Tania felt a surge of hope. This could buy her some time . . . but for what? She could keep running, but she had a feeling that the gargoyle would find her. A plan popped into her head, and Tania decided to go for it. It was now or never.

Tania ducked into the first toolshed she could find. Spiderwebs stuck to her face as she entered the dark space that was crammed with rusty tools and half-empty bags of potting soil. She took the marble from her pocket. Then she crouched down, becoming as still as possible.

The gargoyle wanted his eye back. He had told her so. And he seemed pretty angry that she still had it.

But maybe, Tania thought, *maybe if he thinks I dropped it, he'll leave me alone.*

Tania carefully rolled the marble through a crack in the door, making sure it was clearly visible on the concrete path. She closed the door a bit, making sure there was just enough room to see the marble.

Then she held her breath.

Seconds later, she heard the heavy sounds of the gargoyle as he entered the yard. The gargoyle stomped around angrily.

Then she heard a grunt of satisfaction.

Through the tiny crack, she saw a gray claw reach down and grab the marble. Then the claw disappeared.

He had found it! Tania's heart beat quickly. But the gargoyle hadn't moved.

Finally, after what seemed like forever, she heard the heavy footsteps of the gargoyle as he left the yard.

Tania waited another few minutes before

creeping out of the shed. She decided to head to Grandpa Martin's. She'd have to explain what happened to his birthday present.

That was a close call, Tania admitted to herself. *I guess I should have given that gargoyle his eye when he asked for it!*

THE END

Continued from page 126

"To the trees!" Elias cried.

Lincoln started to run. Elias lifted off, gliding on his leathery wings. He used his strong claws to grab the neck of Lincoln's T-shirt. Then he flew toward the trees. Lincoln's legs dangled as they soared through the air.

Once they reached the trees, Elias dropped Lincoln.

"Hide in the cover of the trees," he instructed. "The sting of these creatures cannot hurt me. I will lure them above the branches and try another charm."

That sounded like a good plan to Lincoln. He just hoped it would work. Lincoln ran deep into the tall pines. Their green branches muffled the sound of the bees somewhat, but Lincoln could still hear them. The sound moved above the trees, just as Elias had said.

The buzzing went on for a few minutes. For a second, everything was silent.

Then, suddenly, something began to fall from the sky. Lincoln covered his head with his hands as tiny chunks of ice—like hailstones—showered him.

But Lincoln soon realized they weren't hailstones at all—they were bees, frozen in ice.

Elias dropped down from the sky with a satisfied smile on his face.

"I used a freezing charm," he said.

"That's pretty awesome," Lincoln said admiringly. He held up one of the frozen bees and examined it. Its stinger looked like a sharp, tiny sword.

"Two battles won," Elias said. "But we must hurry. If we don't reach the chalice soon—"

Elias's smile faded. A look of horror crossed his face.

"It cannot be," he said. "I am turning to stone. But it is not daylight. It can only mean—"

A look of pain crossed the gargoyle's face. His next words were slow and labored. "The . . . Dark . . . One . . . has . . . the . . . chalice."

Then he stopped, frozen in position.

"Elias!" Lincoln cried. He shook the gargoyle, but could not move the cold, still stone.

Lincoln sank to the ground. The Dark Force had won. Tania was missing.

"Help!" he cried into the dark night.

But no one answered.

THE END

Continued from page 36

Slabs of rock fell from the ceiling, crashing behind Tania and Kragg as they ran.

"Where are we going?" Tania yelled above the noise.

Kragg didn't answer. Instead, he pulled her farther into the cavern, into a narrow passageway. As soon as they entered the passageway, a large rock fell behind them, blocking them in.

Then, suddenly, everything was quiet. The cave-in had stopped.

Tania felt glad to be safe—but not at all happy about being trapped inside the cavern.

"Why didn't we go outside, like Elias and Lincoln?" she asked.

"This cave-in was no accident," Kragg said solemnly. "The Dark One is trying to stop us. I had to bring us into this passageway so we can look for the chamber."

"That makes sense," Tania admitted. "So, how are we supposed to find the chamber?"

Kragg frowned. "The map is the surest route. But Elias has the map."

"There was that rhyme, too, wasn't there?" Tania remembered. "Maybe that can help. I think it said something about a snake."

"Where the snake turns, there turn I," Kragg said.

"Right! So all we have to do is look for a snake," Tania said. "I bet this cave is crawling with them."

Tania took off her backpack and dug out a flashlight she had brought along. It had seemed like a good thing to bring to an underground cavern. She switched on the flashlight and aimed it on the floor.

"Hey, snakes," Tania called out. "Come out, come out, wherever you are!" She quickly walked down the passageway.

"Ancient rhymes are usually mysterious," Kragg said as he followed behind her. "It may not be a snake we are looking for. The snake might be symbolic of something."

Tania stopped.

"All I know is that we're in a cave, and snakes like caves," she replied. "Do you have any better ideas?"

Kragg didn't reply right away. Then Tania thought she heard him sigh.

"Carry on," he said.

Tania led the way with her flashlight. Small rocks popped up all along the floor of the passageway, making for a bumpy walk. But there were no signs of snakes—or anything else alive, for that matter.

The air grew colder as they walked deeper and

deeper into the cavern. Tania shivered.

Then something caught her eye.

A small, black shape crawled out from behind one of the rocks. It swiftly wriggled down the path and disappeared from sight.

"A snake!" Tania cried out. She broke into a run.

Wham! Tania tripped over a rock, slamming into the ground. Her flashlight fell out of her hands and rolled a few feet away.

"Stupid rocks," Tania muttered. She jumped to her feet, brushing dirt off her jeans. Kragg had walked over to the fallen flashlight, which leaned on an angle against one of the small rocks. Kragg was looking up at the ceiling.

The flashlight beam illuminated a stalactite hanging from the roof. Tania thought it looked like an icicle, but she knew from science class that it was really a mineral—calcium carbonate. The mineral dripped down from the ceiling over time, forming unusual shapes.

This stalactite was shaped exactly like a snake. Just beyond it, Tania saw the entrance to a new passageway.

Kragg said quietly, "This may be the symbolic snake we are looking for. Remember the words of the rhyme. *Where the snake turns, there turn I.* We must follow the snake."

But Tania was stubborn. "But I saw a snake! A real snake," she said. "And it went straight down the path. We should follow the *real* snake—not something that just looks like a snake."

If Tania and Kragg follow the real snake, go to page 89.

If Tania and Kragg follow the stalactite, go to page 83.

Continued from page 78

"Help me with that ladder over there," Tania said.

Lincoln sighed and did as he was told.

"I don't understand you, Tania," he said. "Are you sure you're all right? Maybe you're in shock from seeing that gargoyle last night."

"It's no big deal," Tania replied. "There's no one around. I bet nobody even knows that this gargoyle is back here. They're sure not going to miss one measly eye. Besides, it's like we're doing . . . historical research."

Lincoln didn't reply, but he seemed satisfied with the answer. He and Tania propped the ladder up underneath the gargoyle's ledge. Tania patted the front pocket of her jeans to make sure that the penknife she had brought was still there. To her surprise, the black marble in her pocket felt unusually warm.

Then Tania began to climb as Lincoln held the ladder steady. It didn't do much good. Each rung creaked loudly under her weight. She had set down her foot on the last rung when . . .

CRACK!

The rung snapped in two. Tania lost her footing and tumbled down the ladder.

She heard another cracking sound when she

hit the ground, but it wasn't a broken bone. Tania had a sinking feeling she knew what it was. She reached into her pocket and pulled out the penknife . . . and a handful of black dust and cracked glass. She had broken the black marble!

"You okay?" Lincoln asked.

"Yeah, I guess," Tania said. She wasn't hurt, just disappointed. The book had said that the four marbles together had amazing power—but now one was lost forever.

"We might as well go home, Lincoln," Tania said.

As they walked home, Tania wondered if she really *did* see a gargoyle in her room the night before.

Maybe Grandpa Martin was right, it was probably just an owl. Or was it? Tania decided she really didn't want to find out.

THE END

Continued from page 16

Tania thought about it. Striking out a batter was one thing. But fighting a force of evil as old as time? She might be more than a "mere girl," but she wasn't a superhero.

"I'm sorry, Kragg," Tania said. "I think you might have been right before. This sounds like a big job—too big for someone like me."

Kragg nodded. "I understand," he said.

"I can still look in the Yellow Pages, if you want," Tania suggested helpfully. "Just because I've never heard of an alchemist doesn't mean there isn't one around."

"I will continue my search," Kragg said. "I am sure we will find a human who can help us. But, first, there is something I must do."

"What's that?" Tania asked.

Kragg looked into Tania's eyes. Immediately, Tania felt frozen, unable to move.

Uh-oh, Tania thought.

Beams of light flashed from Kragg's glittering, black eyes. The bright light blinded Tania. She started to feel dizzy . . .

Tania blinked. She was sitting on the edge of her bed, but she wasn't sure why. She remembered that Lincoln came over to do homework. She showed him the black marble she had bought at

Sebastian Cream's Junk Shop. And then . . .

She couldn't remember. It was the oddest thing. Had she fallen asleep? She felt a little drowsy.

The marble! It had something to do with the marble. Tania searched her room. Where had she put it? It wasn't on her desk, or in her backpack.

I bet Lincoln took it, Tania realized. *That rat! First, he sticks up for Jennifer. Now, this. I am going to give him a piece of my mind tomorrow.*

Outside the window, Kragg the gargoyle frowned, hidden in the shadows.

"I am sorry you could not help us, Tania," he whispered. "You might have been the one."

Then he vanished into the night.

THE END

Continued from page 78

Tania looked at the ladder again, but decided it didn't look sturdy enough. She checked to make sure she still had her penknife tucked in her pocket. Then she started to climb the walls to reach the gargoyle.

"Tania, this is nuts!" Lincoln called up after her.

"Stop worrying," she shot back. "I bet nobody even knows this thing is up here. They're definitely not going to notice if it's missing an eye. Besides, it's like we're doing historical research." That's how she'd explain things to Grandpa, anyway.

Tania had done lots of indoor rock climbing at the Bleaktown Sports Center, so scaling the church wall was pretty easy. She swung herself up on the ledge next to the gargoyle. There was just enough space for her to squeeze in on the gargoyle's right side.

Seeing the gargoyle up close made Tania shiver. Even though it was made out of stone, she could definitely imagine it springing to life at any moment. She carefully reached out and tapped the gargoyle's back.

Nothing happened.

Tania let out a breath and took out her penknife. Getting the eye shouldn't be too hard—but which eye was the magic eye? Tania took the black marble from her pocket and held it up to compare.

Both of the gargoyle's eyes were milky white. But only the gargoyle's left eye shone—as if it was lit from somewhere deep within—just like the black marble.

That had to be the one. Tania leaned over the gargoyle's face and slid the dull blade of the knife around the marble. After a few seconds of prying, the marble flew out of the gargoyle's stone eye socket.

Tania reached out to grab it, but missed by a mile.

"Lincoln!" she yelled. "Catch it!"

Tania stashed away the penknife and the black marble and scurried back down the wall. She found Lincoln kneeling on the ground, searching through the grass.

"Why didn't you catch it?" she asked crossly.

"I wasn't ready!" Lincoln said. "Besides, I saw where it fell. It's right here."

Lincoln held out his palm. The white marble rested in the center.

Immediately, Tania felt the black marble move inside her pocket. It felt like it was moving on its own. She quickly took it out of her pocket.

The white marble on Lincoln's palm began to

roll down to his fingertips, toward Tania's hand. The black marble rolled down Tania's hand toward the white marble. When they were just inches apart, they both began to glow more brightly and deeply than they had before.

"Wow," Tania said. "There's definitely something weird going on here. Why are the marbles moving toward each other?"

"Maybe they're magnetic or something," Lincoln suggested.

Tania shook her head. "No way. That legend is true. And once we get all four marbles, we'll be able to prove it. We'll be famous!"

"You think?" Lincoln asked.

"Of course," Tania said. "The four marbles are supposed to have amazing powers when they're all together. I bet we'll be able to do anything we want!"

That seemed to convince Lincoln. "When do you want to go look for the silver marble?" he asked.

"Right now!" Tania said.

"But don't you have softball practice?" Lincoln asked.

"That's not important," Tania said. "I can miss one lousy practice." *Besides, everyone will be too busy bowing at Jennifer's feet to notice I'm gone,* she finished silently to herself.

"Well, I'm not exactly sure how to get there . . ." Lincoln said.

"We'll find it!" Tania snapped. "Honestly, Lincoln, are you with me on this, or what?"

"I'm with you," he replied. "I just think we should look tomorrow."

If Tania and Lincoln look for the silver marble tomorrow, go to page 37.

If Tania and Lincoln decide not to wait, go to page 120.

Continued from page 107

Turning into the alley seemed like the easiest way to go. Tania changed course and veered left.

The narrow alley acted as a connector to Willow Street, which formed the top of a "T" at the alley's end. Tania made another left, which would take her back toward Grandpa Martin's—and safety.

She ran straight down the middle of the wide street. It took a few seconds to realize that she didn't hear the heavy sound of the gargoyle's running feet any longer. *Is it possible that I lost him?* She risked a quick look behind her.

Tania didn't see the gargoyle behind her.

She saw him above her. The gargoyle had taken flight on his leathery wings. He was directly above her now. Tania watched in horror as he swooped down and landed directly in front of her, blocking her.

There was nowhere to run.

"Give me back my eye!" the gargoyle growled.

Tania reached into her pocket and grabbed the marble. Then she had an idea.

I'll just freeze him again, she thought. *I'll freeze him and leave the marble here. Then I can get away safely.*

Tania was about to throw the marble down, but the gargoyle was suddenly in front of her, his lone black eye glittering angrily.

"Not again," he said, grabbing her wrist. With his other claw, he took the marble and stuck it back in his empty eye socket.

Tania had never been so frightened in her life. The gargoyle's face was inches from hers. Up close, she could see that his skin looked like gray leather. The touch of his claw felt like ice.

"S-S-S-Sorry," Tania stammered. "It's just that you scared me the other night, and—"

"You are nothing but a thief," the gargoyle snarled. "A thief who knows my secrets."

"But I didn't steal your eye!" Tania protested. "I bought it in a shop. I bet the weird guy who owns the shop stole it."

"Enough," the gargoyle said firmly. "Now you must pay."

Tania struggled to get out of the gargoyle's grasp, but he was too strong. Helpless, she saw the gargoyle's eyes glow from within. Then a light shot out from them, enveloping her.

Now her whole body felt like ice. The gargoyle let go now, and Tania tried to run, but realized, strangely, that she couldn't.

Then she noticed her hand. It was in front of her face, palm open as it had been when the gargoyle took the marble.

Her whole hand had turned to stone. Tania tried to look down at the rest of her body, but she couldn't move her head at all. She watched as the gargoyle smiled, satisfied, and then flew off into the night.

Tania tried with all her might to scream, but no sound escaped from her stone face.

THE END

Continued from page 99

Lincoln didn't feel confident enough to try to trick Tania. Instead, he quickly reached out and tried to take the chalice from her.

But before he could even get close, Tania reached out and grabbed his arm. Her grip felt strong—stronger than the grip of a twelve-year-old girl.

"How dare you try to interfere?" Tania snapped. Then she pushed Lincoln with tremendous force. He went hurling backward and slammed into the back wall of the cave.

"Strength and power shall be mine!" Tania shouted. Before Lincoln could rise to his feet, she drank from the chalice.

"We are doomed," Elias said wearily.

The effects after Tania drank from the chalice were immediate. Lincoln watched, frozen in horror, as Tania transformed before his eyes. Her spine and limbs stretched and twisted into hideous shapes. Her soft, brown eyes turned bright green; her mouth stretched until it became a square snout filled with sharp teeth. Her skin became green and leathery. Her curly, brown hair transformed into a mass of snakes.

It all happened in seconds. There was no trace left of Tania. A hideous monster stood in her place, practically filling the chamber.

"Tania?" Lincoln felt like he was dreaming.

He felt Elias grab the back of his shirt and drag him out of the chamber.

"We can't just leave Tania there!" Lincoln protested.

"Nothing can help her now," Elias said. "The Dark One has won. My people are doomed. All because of the weakness of humans."

Elias's words stung, but Lincoln knew he was right.

Lincoln had failed miserably.

THE END

Continued from page 22

Suddenly, Lincoln changed his mind.

"What am I saying?" he said, slapping his fore-head. "We're chasing after gargoyles that come to life. Why would we want to do that?"

"To prove that it's real," Tania countered. "I know what I saw in my bedroom. I want to find out what this is all about."

Tania had another reason, too, but she kept it to herself. The book had said that together, the four marbles possessed amazing powers. Well, she already had one marble. She wondered what would happen if she found all four . . .

Grandpa Martin frowned. "It might not be about anything, Tania. I believe you saw something in your room. I'm just not convinced it was a living gargoyle."

"It matches the legend, doesn't it?" Tania pointed out.

Grandpa nodded. "Yes, it does," he admitted.

Tania turned to Lincoln. "Besides, we'll go in the daylight, when the gargoyles are sleeping or whatever. What could go wrong?"

Lincoln didn't look convinced, but he agreed to meet Tania at her church the next morning.

The early-morning light cast a soft glow on Bleaktown as they rode their bikes. *It makes the streets, with their box-like houses and shops, look almost pretty,* Tania thought. Usually Bleaktown looked as bleak as its name.

It didn't take long to get to the church. Tania knew, from passing by its cornerstone every time she entered, that it was one of the oldest buildings in town. Gray blocks of stone formed the walls of the large, square structure. Colorful, arch-shaped stained-glass windows broke up the dull gray on the side walls. A weather-worn bell waited in the steeple to be rung on Sunday morning. And a spiky, black metal fence surrounded the grounds, including a small cemetery with crumbling stones on the left side.

"So, where's this gargoyle?" Lincoln asked, climbing off his bike.

"I'm not sure, but it's got to be here," Tania said. "Let's look around."

They parked their bikes outside the fence and circled the building. Tania shaded her eyes from the rising sun and looked up.

Then she saw it. On the back wall, a gargoyle statue sat high over the back door, resting on a ledge shaped like a half-moon. This one looked a bit friendlier than the black-eyed gargoyle—it had long, rounded ears that came to a point, a round, squashed nose, a grinning smile—and two white marbles in its eyes.

"There it is," Tania whispered.

"Cool," Lincoln said. "Well, we found it. What now?"

"Now, we take out its eye," Tania said matter-of-factly.

Lincoln looked startled. "What?"

"It's the only way to know if the legend is true," she said. "I've just got to climb up there and get it."

"Do what you want," Lincoln said, shrugging his head.

Tania looked for a way up. She saw a rickety-looking ladder nearby. That might work. But she could also try to climb up to the gargoyle using the cracks and crevices in the stone wall.

If Tania tries the ladder, go to page 63.

If Tania tries to climb up to the gargoyle, go to page 67.

Continued from page 36

It all happened so fast that when Lincoln thought about it later, it seemed like a blur. There had been a rumbling sound in the cave. Then he felt a cold hand grab his sleeve. Rocks had started falling all around him. The next thing he knew, he was outside the cave with the gargoyle Kragg had called Elias.

And everyone else was trapped inside.

"Tania!" Lincoln cried. He broke away from Elias and ran toward the mouth of the cave, which was blocked with fallen rocks and boulders.

But Elias grabbed his arm once again.

"There is nothing you can do," Elias said. "I saw Kragg grab hold of her. He is very strong. She will be safe."

"But what about the others?" Lincoln asked. "The other gargoyles."

"My brothers are strong, too. Stronger than the stone that traps them," Elias said. "They will find a way out. But, until they do, the chalice is in danger."

Elias held up the ancient map that he had brought to the cavern. "I must try to find the chalice before the Dark One finds it," he said. Then he turned and began to walk down the path.

Lincoln stood still for a minute, completely confused. Tania was trapped inside the mountain. It was dark out, and the Dark One was roaming around here somewhere. Elias wasn't exactly the friendliest gargoyle in the world, but at least he made Lincoln feel safe.

"Hey, wait up!" Lincoln called, catching up to the gargoyle. "I thought you needed a human to go into the chamber with you. You should take me with you."

Elias sighed. He stopped and turned to face Lincoln.

"You are right, human," he said. "But you must do as I say."

"My name's Lincoln," the boy replied. "And I'll do whatever you want. I just want to find Tania and get out of here."

"Very well," Elias said. He turned and kept walking.

Lincoln ran to catch up to the gargoyle's side. "How do you know where you're going?" Lincoln said. "It's pitch-black out here. I wish we had Tania's flashlight."

Elias snorted. "We are creatures of the night. We do not need light in the dark. Just follow me and keep quiet."

Lincoln followed behind Elias for a few minutes. The gargoyle looked at the map, then walked off the path and hiked up the mountain.

The climb was steep, and Lincoln huffed and puffed as he walked. They had walked on for what seemed like an hour when Lincoln finally spoke up.

"I thought the chamber was underground," he said. "Why are we climbing the mountain?"

"There is a way to enter the chamber from above," Elias said. "The map shows the way. Now no more talking."

Lincoln didn't know how much more he could take. "Are you sure?" asked Lincoln. "We've been walking forever!"

"Quiet!" snapped Elias.

"You know, you're pretty mean for a—"

A thunderous sound filled the sky above. Lincoln looked up, and in the moonlight he saw a huge flock of black birds flying toward the mountain. As they got closer, he could see that they were aimed directly at him and Elias.

The birds' eyes gleamed yellow in the moonlight. Their black beaks came to sharp points. They definitely did not look friendly.

"Messengers of the Dark One," Elias said solemnly. Then he closed his eyes and began to chant in a strange language.

Lincoln couldn't believe it. What was Elias doing? Desperate, he scanned the surroundings for cover. Nearby, he saw what looked like a large hollow in the ground.

It beat standing around, waiting to be pecked to death by birds. Lincoln sprinted for the hole.

Behind him, he heard Elias yell:

"Foolish boy! Come back here!"

If Lincoln keeps running, go to page 41.
If Lincoln listens to Elias, go to page 123.

Continued from page 62

"All gargoyles have a connection to the life force," Kragg said. "When I look at this stalactite, I feel something in the core of my being. I think following it is the right thing to do."

Tania couldn't argue with that. "All right," she said. "But if we don't find anything, we should turn back and go my way."

"Agreed," Kragg said.

Tania shone the flashlight ahead as they walked. "So now that we answered that part of the rhyme, what are we looking for now?" she asked. "I can't remember the next part."

"To the water's edge I fly," Kragg said.

"Boy, you gargoyles have good memories," Tania said. "So, I guess that means we're looking for water?"

"That would seem so," Kragg said.

"Real water, or something shaped like water?" Tania asked.

"I do not know," Kragg said. "Ancient rhymes are very—"

"Mysterious, I know," Tania interrupted.

The two walked in silence for a while. Then Tania spoke up.

"So, tell me more about this Dark One," she said. "That cave-in it caused was pretty nasty. I guess it's pretty powerful, huh?"

"Yes, it is," Kragg said. "I do not know much about the Dark One. Except that it is very, very old. Perhaps older than time."

"There's got to be more," Tania said. "I mean, what does it look like?"

"It can take any shape it desires," Kragg said. "It uses deception to corrupt the hearts of men."

"Any shape?" Tania asked. "Like, a giant monster or something?"

"Long ago, yes," Kragg replied. "But its power waned once the gargoyles were created. Our very existence keeps the Dark One in the shadows. But without the life force . . ."

Tania understood. When Kragg had asked her to come to the chamber, she had thought of it as some kind of an adventure. But now it seemed really important to succeed. This Dark One could cause real trouble.

Suddenly, she remembered Lincoln.

"Do you think Lincoln's all right?" she asked, feeling worried. "What if the Dark One is after him?"

"The Dark One is only interested in the chamber," Kragg assured her. "If it comes after anyone, it will be us."

Tania shivered at Kragg's words, but she kept walking. There was no turning back now.

Soon, Tania heard a sound.

"Do you hear that?" she asked. "It sounds like water."

Tania quickened her pace. Soon, something glittered in the light of her flashlight.

They had reached a stream. Dark water flowed across the path, which then veered to both the right and left.

"To the water's edge I fly. Then travel to where the secrets lie," Kragg finished the rhyme.

"So, I guess the rhyme was about real water," Tania said. "We just have to follow it to the chamber. But which way do we go?"

Kragg was silent for a minute. Finally, he said, "I do not know."

"Then we've got to pick one way and hope we're right," Tania said.

If Tania and Kragg travel downstream, go to page 43.

If Tania and Kragg travel upstream, go to page 117.

Continued from page 131

Tania didn't back down. If they could get rid of the stone-carver guy somehow, she could figure out how to use the marbles on her own. She just wouldn't use them for evil purposes, that's all.

"Just act casual," Tania said. "I'll take care of it."

Lincoln sighed. He and Tania broke their huddle. She faced Talbot, smiling.

"We'd be happy to help you," she said. "NOT!"

Tania charged at the ghostly stone carver like a football player charging the quarterback. But she passed right through his body, which felt like a clammy fog. Her skin felt damp and slimy.

She turned to face Talbot. There had to be some way to attack him. She expected him to be angry, but instead he was smiling widely.

"Thank you," he said. "For sharing your life force with me. I'm feeling stronger already."

Tania realized that Talbot looked less filmy somehow. A pale, flesh color had appeared on his face and hands, and his eyes were now a watery blue.

"Strong enough, in fact," Talbot said, "that I believe I am able to handle the marbles on my own."

Talbot held out his palm. The four marbles,

which had still been swirling all around him, moved toward his hand. One by one, they plopped into his palm. But, instead of the marbles passing straight through, as they had done with Tania, they rested there safely.

"Marvelous," Talbot muttered. "Simply marvelous."

Lincoln tugged on Tania's arm.

"Let's get out of here while we have a chance," he whispered.

Talbot had overheard him. "I'm afraid you two aren't going anywhere," he said. He quickly whispered something to the marbles. They began to bounce rapidly in his hand. Before Lincoln and Tania could react, beams of white, black, silver, and gold light exploded from the marbles.

Tania felt the strangest tingling sensation when the rays of light hit her. She started to turn and run, but, to her horror, she felt she could not move.

Panicked, Tania tried moving her arms, her hands, her neck. Nothing. The best she could do was move her eyes. She saw Lincoln next to her, frozen like a statue.

Talbot floated closer. "Not bad," he said. "But not quite enough. We will have to try again."

Tania discovered that she could still speak.

"What are you doing to us?" she asked.

"You two know my secret," Talbot said. "I thought you were sorcerers of a like mind. But your attack proved me wrong. So, now I must dispose of you . . . the same way I dispose of all my enemies."

Tania's stomach lurched. "You're going to turn us to stone?"

Talbot grinned. "Why, of course. You should feel privileged. It has not happened to many people."

"We won't tell anybody!" Lincoln wailed. "We promise. Please set us free!"

"Now, that wouldn't be any fun, would it?" Talbot said. He began whispering to the marbles again. Once again, they bounced on his hand, faster this time.

Then the light flashed.

It was like getting hit with a bag of bricks. Tania felt a huge force slam against her. Her feet and legs felt heavy. Looking down, she saw that they had turned to stone . . . and the stone was creeping up her body.

Tania looked at Lincoln. He had already transformed. He looked like a statue, his face frozen in a scream.

"Noooooooo!" Tania yelled.

But it was too late.

THE END

Continued from page 62

Kragg hesitated.

"Listen, you need a human to help you, right?" Tania asked. "Well, I'm your human, and I say we follow the snake. If we don't find anything, we'll turn back. I promise."

"That is reasonable," Kragg said. "Let us find your snake."

Tania continued down the path as Kragg followed behind. They hadn't gone far before the path came to a dead end.

"Drat!" Tania muttered. She shone her flashlight beam against the stone wall. At the bottom, she saw the small, black snake curled around a rock.

"Maybe there's a secret passage or something," Tania suggested. "Let me take a look before we turn back."

Tania walked up to the wall and began pounding on it with her fists. Nothing.

Then she got an idea. She leaned down toward the rock that the snake had curled around. Maybe there was some kind of secret lever or something.

"Nice snake," she said, cautiously lowering her hand.

The snake's head reared back, and it hissed. Tania jumped back, startled.

Then the snake began to grow. Tania watched, horrified, as its dark shape got larger and larger, until the snake towered above Kragg.

Then the snake began to speak.

"You have failed, old one," it hissed.

Kragg moved between Tania and the snake. "It is the Dark One," he said. "It can take any form it chooses."

"And now I choose to seal your doom," hissed the snake.

The cavern trembled. Before Tania and Kragg could make a move, a huge boulder rolled down the passageway, trapping them between it and the wall.

"Your life force will be mine!" cried the snake.

Then it disappeared.

Still trembling, Tania shone her flashlight on the boulder, then on the walls.

"We are trapped," Kragg said simply.

Tania didn't know what to say. She ran over to the large rocks and began pounding on them. "Help! Help!" she cried.

But no one answered her cries. No one at all.

THE END

Continued from page 22

"Let's look for the silver marble tomorrow," Tania said. "Since the park is across town, we'd better go after softball practice. I don't think I'll have time to go before then."

Grandpa Martin walked them both home. In the morning, Tania watched some cartoons, then went to softball practice. Everyone fussed over Jennifer Delgado again, and Tania was in a pretty bad mood by the time Lincoln showed up on his bicycle.

"Come on!" Lincoln said. "I'm dying to find one of those gargoyles."

"I've got to eat something first," Tania said. "I've been running around all morning."

Now it was Lincoln's turn to tap his foot as Tania got a hot dog from the cart in the baseball park. When she finished her last bite, she jumped on her bike and followed Lincoln.

It was already afternoon by the time they got started. They rode through Bleaktown's downtown area, which was crowded with cars and shoppers. They rode past Bleaktown Park and Town Hall. They kept riding until they reached an old abandoned warehouse. Lincoln got off his bike and frowned.

"That's funny," said Lincoln. "The directions said it was right here."

"Let me see them," demanded Tania.

Lincoln reached into his pocket and fumbled for the piece of paper. "I must have left it home," he admitted.

"Lincoln!" Tania said, annoyed.

Lincoln shrugged. "Sorry," he said. "I'm sure the park is around here somewhere."

Lincoln hopped back on his bike and started pedaling. Suddenly, there was a loud, popping sound. Lincoln's tire had been flattened by a nail.

They had to wheel their bikes downtown so Lincoln could get the wheel fixed at the bike shop. The sun was starting to sink in the sky— Tania knew her mom would be worried about her—but Lincoln persisted. They were almost there.

This time, they rode down leafy streets lined with houses a lot fancier and bigger than Tania and Lincoln's neighborhood.

"This is where my aunt lives!" Lincoln said. "We're getting close."

But now it was dark, and the streetlights turned on all at once. Tania started to wheel around.

"Sorry, Lincoln," she said. "We'll try tomorrow."

"GIVE ME BACK MY EYE!"

Tania almost fell off her bike. The gargoyle

from last night had jumped in front of her, his single black eye glowing angrily.

This time, Tania didn't hesitate. She fished the eye out of her pocket and threw it to the gargoyle.

The gargoyle grunted, lifted off on his leathery wings, and disappeared into the night.

Tania turned to find Lincoln, as still as a statue, gripping his bike handles for dear life.

"So, now do you believe me?" Tania asked shakily.

"I th-th-think so," Lincoln whispered, stuttering.

The two friends slowly hopped on their bikes, and rode home in silence.

THE END

Tania suddenly felt awful. She didn't deserve these cheers. Using the marble to make Jennifer look bad and herself look good hadn't been right at all.

On the bus ride home, Tania sat by herself way in the back, sulking the whole way. She walked home alone and found Lincoln sitting on her front steps.

"Don't say it," Tania said. "I feel bad enough already."

"Just take the marble back to where you got it," Lincoln advised. "Then this will all be over."

Tania nodded. "You're right. I'll go tomorrow after school."

And Tania kept her word. She got lost again, trying to find Wary Lane, but she soon found the strange shop. She found Mr. Cream with his head stuck inside the open jaws of an old, stuffed tiger. He immediately popped out when Tania stepped inside.

"Dropped my glasses," he said as a way of explanation. Then he straightened the glasses on his face and smiled.

"Ah, Tania," he said. "Did your grandfather enjoy the marble?"

Tania reached into her pocket and took it out.

"I didn't give it to him," she said. She took a deep breath. How much did she want to tell Mr. Cream? "I . . . used it myself."

A frown crossed Mr. Cream's face. "You don't mean you used it to freeze time? Why, that's very dangerous."

How did he know? Tania wondered. But his comment had her worried. "Dangerous? How?"

"Humans aren't strong enough to use the marble's power for long," he explained. "If they use it once too often, they will become frozen in time themselves. Very nasty business."

Tania felt relieved. Then she had returned the marble just in time. It was a good thing she had listened to Lincoln.

"So, would you like to exchange this, or have your money back?" Mr. Cream asked.

"Money back, please," Tania said quickly.

She wasn't about to buy another item from Mr. Cream's crazy shop. Who knows what kind of trouble that might bring!

THE END

Continued from page 126

"Head for the cover of the rock!" Elias shouted.

Lincoln didn't hesitate. He sprinted toward the overhanging rock as fast as he could run. The sound of the buzzing bees seemed to grow louder with each step.

Elias flew to the overhang and reached the rock just seconds before Lincoln. He grabbed Lincoln and pulled him inside.

The strong gargoyle sent Lincoln tumbling to the ground. Lincoln braced himself to hit the ground, but, instead, he felt his body falling into a void.

Before he could cry out, he landed with a thud a few feet below.

"Hey!" The fall knocked the wind out of Lincoln. After a few seconds, he sat up, brushing dirt off his jeans. Looking up, he saw Elias's head peering down at him. Apparently, he had fallen into some kind of hole in the ground.

"What did you do that for?" Lincoln asked.

The gargoyle's gold eyes glittered in the darkness. He looked as though he was going to reply, but then he suddenly stopped. He seemed to have spotted something.

"You may have stumbled on something useful, human," Elias said. He jumped down through the hole, landing on his feet.

"What do you mean?" Lincoln asked.

Elias pointed behind Lincoln.

"I believe we may have found the chamber."

Lincoln turned around. It was too dark to see anything clearly, but a shaft of moonlight illuminated a stone wall. The shape of a circle was carved into the stone. In the center of the circle was an imprint of what looked like a human hand. Some kind of strange writing circled the handprint.

"That's the chamber?" Lincoln asked.

"The carvings on the stone are written in an ancient language," Elias said. "They say, in part, 'Only one who is human born shall enter.' I never understood that rule. What kind of fool would leave humans in charge of something so important?"

Lincoln took a deep breath. The time had come when he could finally show Elias that humans weren't idiots. He stepped toward the door.

Then he stopped, puzzled. How was he supposed to get in? There was no handle.

"Put your hand in the imprint," Elias said impatiently.

Embarrassed, Lincoln pressed his hand into the imprint. The stone circle slid to the left with a grinding sound. Lincoln climbed through the hole.

He gasped. Tania stood in the center of the chamber, holding a silver chalice in her hand. A soft light glowed from inside the chalice, illuminating the tiny room. On the opposite wall, Lincoln saw Kragg standing outside an open door.

"Tania! I can't believe we found you!" Lincoln cried, running toward his friend. "I thought you were stuck in the cave-in."

Tania didn't reply. Lincoln leaned over and looked in the chalice.

"Hey, is that the life force of the gargoyles in there?" Lincoln asked excitedly. " 'Cause we should get it to the gargoyles, quick. The Dark One is out there, and he's got evil birds and bees and—"

Tania laughed, but it didn't sound like Tania at all. Her voice sounded old and deep. Lincoln noticed for the first time that there was a strange look in Tania's eyes. It was as though Tania had left her body—and somebody else had taken over.

"The life force is mine now, Lincoln!" Tania said. "Once I drink it, I will become as strong and powerful as the gargoyles!"

"What are you talking about?" Lincoln knew something definitely wasn't right.

Then Kragg called out from the other side of the chamber. "She is under the control of the

Dark One, Lincoln! You must stop her from drinking the life force!"

Behind him, Lincoln heard Elias snort.

Lincoln tried to pull himself together. It was up to him now to save everything. He had to stop Tania.

But how?

If he tried to grab the chalice away from her, he would risk spilling the life force. He had to trick Tania into giving up the chalice somehow. But that was risky, too. It might not work.

If Lincoln tries to trick Tania into giving up the life force, go to page 139.

If Lincoln tries to grab the chalice from Tania, go to page 74.

Hearing Lincoln's voice brought Tania back to reality. What was she doing, listening to some evil guy? He was probably trying to trick her or something.

Then something occurred to her. She had the marbles in her hand . . . but Talbot wasn't trying to take them from her or attack her. Maybe he couldn't do that in his ghostly form. That's probably why he was trying to trick her.

Maybe they didn't have to smash the marbles after all. Maybe they could just take them. It was worth a try.

"Lincoln, get out of here!" Tania cried. She jumped on her bike and began to pedal as fast as she could. She heard Lincoln struggling to get on his bike behind her. She looked back to see Talbot. He looked angry, but he wasn't coming after them.

"You will pay for this!" he yelled.

And then his ghostly body vanished.

Still, Tania didn't slow down. She zipped down Main Street and down the side streets, not stopping until she got to Grandpa Martin's house. She ran up the steps and pounded on the door. Her grandfather opened it right away.

"Tania, what's the matter?" he asked.

Tania wasn't sure where to start. Catching her breath, she sat down on the couch and put the marbles on the coffee table.

"You found the four marbles?" Grandpa asked, raising an eyebrow.

"We found them all," Lincoln said, bursting through the front door. "And then they started floating around, and then this evil stone-carver guy appeared, and he tried to make Tania evil, and . . ."

Grandpa Martin held up his hand. "Slow down, now. I'm going to make us some dinner. You two call your parents and tell them where you are. Then we'll sort all of this out."

Fifteen minutes later, the three of them sat at the tiny table in Grandpa Martin's kitchen, eating bowls of vegetable soup from a can and munching on grilled cheese sandwiches. Tania had placed the marbles in the center of the table.

"So," Grandpa Martin said. "Tell me what happened. Slowly, please."

Tania and Lincoln began telling the story, interrupting each other the whole time. They told Grandpa how they had found the white marble at the church, the silver marble at the park, and the gold marble at the library. They told him how the marbles glowed and danced when they were all together, and how Talbot had appeared. (Although in Lincoln's version, the stone carver had vampire fangs and wore a black cape.) Then Tania explained how she had taken the marbles from Talbot.

Grandpa Martin looked thoughtful. He didn't say, "You and your imagination!" or "Stop telling stories," like Tania's mother or father would have. Instead, he said, "I believe you."

"But," he added. "I do have a question. Why aren't the marbles glowing or dancing now?"

Tania frowned. "I don't know," she said. "Maybe they're, like, tired or something."

Grandpa patted his face with a napkin and stood up from the table. "I'm going to check my library and see what I can find out about this Talbot fellow," he said. "You two clean up the dishes."

"Sure, Grandpa," Lincoln and Tania said together. But just as they stood up from the table, the marbles began to glow brightly again.

"Grandpa! Look!" Tania cried.

The marbles slowly lifted off the table, and once again began to move around in a circle.

"Well, I'll be . . . " Grandpa Martin exclaimed.

The marbles swirled off the table, floated across the room, and paused in front of the back door.

"It looks like the marbles want to go outside,"

Lincoln said.

"Then we should let them," Grandpa said. He opened the back door.

Tania hadn't realized it, but night had fallen while they were eating dinner. The marbles floated out into the dark. Tania, Lincoln, and Grandpa all followed the marbles into Grandpa's tiny backyard, which held his weather-beaten rocking chair, his rosebushes—and four gargoyles!

Lincoln, Tania, and Grandpa Martin all screamed. The four gargoyles sat in a row, facing the house. One gargoyle had one black eye; one had one white eye; one had one silver eye; and one had one gold eye. Tania recognized them all. The marbles floated toward the gargoyles and then stopped, hovering in the air.

"We have come for our eyes," said the black-eyed gargoyle.

"We're sorry about all of this," Tania said quickly. "We heard the marbles had powers. And then Talbot appeared, and—"

"Talbot!" said the gargoyle. They all looked suddenly agitated. "That is the fiend who turned us into this form."

"Talbot told us he used the power of the marbles to transform you," Tania said. "Maybe they can turn you back."

"You may be right, Tania," Grandpa said.

"And how do we do that?" snapped the white-eyed gargoyle.

Everyone was silent for a moment. Then Lincoln blurted out, "Why don't you ask the marbles?"

Tania thought that sounded silly, but Grandpa said, "Excellent idea, Lincoln."

Grandpa stepped up to the marbles and started talking to them. The marbles began to swirl in the air, glowing more and more brightly.

Suddenly, the yard exploded in a blast of light. Tania shaded her eyes from the brightness. When she opened her eyes again, she saw an amazing sight.

Four men stood where the four gargoyles had stood before. They all wore old-fashioned clothing.

"The curse is over!" one man exclaimed.

"Fascinating," Grandpa Martin said. "Gentlemen, I think we have a lot to discuss. Come on in and have some dinner."

Tania and Lincoln watched, dumbfounded, as Grandpa led the transformed gargoyles into his house.

As Tania and Lincoln followed Grandpa and the gargoyles into the house, they looked at each other quietly.

"Um, this is so weird," whispered Lincoln.

"I know," Tania responded, sighing.

The last three days had been some of the strangest days Tania had ever experienced. And it had all started at Sebastian Cream's Junk Shop. Maybe the storeowner could tell her what all of this had been about. Tania decided to pay Sebastian Cream a visit first thing in the morning.

Go to page 142.

Continued from page 116

Tania wasn't sure what to do. She thought about it all afternoon, while she helped her mom and dad clean the garage. She thought about it all during dinner.

Finally, she decided that Lincoln was right. Sure, it had been fun seeing Jennifer mess up during practice—but a part of her felt sorry for Jennifer, and ashamed of herself.

"I'm going to see Grandpa Martin," Tania told her parents, who were sitting in the living room watching TV.

"Tell him we'll see him for brunch tomorrow," said Mrs. Robbins.

Tania nodded and headed out into the night. Since she had turned twelve, her mom and dad had let her walk to Grandpa's house alone. It was only a few blocks away. Grandpa's birthday wasn't for a week yet, but Tania would give him the marble early, and maybe try to explain things to him. Of all people, she knew he would understand.

Tania took the marble out of her pocket and let it roll around in her hand while she walked. She passed a bunch of kids playing wiffle ball on Elm Street. But when she turned onto Maple Street, she saw no one outside.

Then, out of nowhere, Tania heard the sound

of heavy footsteps behind her.

That's weird, Tania thought, her heart pounding a little faster. There couldn't be anyone behind her. Unless someone had dropped from the sky . . .

Tania stopped. It couldn't be. She slowly turned her head.

The one-eyed gargoyle was charging after her, a look of fury on his face.

Tania's feet started moving on their own. She charged down Maple and then turned down the first side street she came to. Up ahead, she saw that the street ended in a dead end.

Panicked, Tania looked up and down the dark street for the best place to run. She saw the entrance to an alley up on the left. That might work. Or, she could try cutting across some backyards and maybe losing the gargoyle that way.

If Tania cuts across some backyards, go to page 54.

If Tania runs into the alley, go to page 71.

Continued from page 116

Tania couldn't bring herself to give up the marble just yet. All day Sunday, she plotted new ways to use the marble in Monday's game. It might not have been a big deal when Jennifer messed up in practice, but if everyone saw her lose an important game, Tania would go back to being the star player again—just like she deserved to be.

When the school bell rang Monday morning, nearly every kid in sixth grade was talking about the game. The Bleaktown Spiders were playing their top rivals, the Woodside Coyotes. Both teams were tied for first place. Whoever won this game would win a guaranteed slot in the finals.

After school, the team boarded the bus for Woodside Field. The field in Bleaktown was old and unkempt. The peeling wooden bleachers could give you splinters if you weren't careful, and brown patches dotted the grass in the outfield.

But Woodside Field was something else. Shining metal and fiberglass bleachers flanked a baseball diamond made of perfectly manicured, emerald-green grass. The Coyotes wore real uniforms and cleats, not just the team T-shirts and shorts that the Spiders wore. As the bus pulled up to the field, the Coyotes were all in the infield, tossing the ball to one another.

As she stepped off the bus, Tania remembered how much she hated the Coyotes and forgot all about her bad feelings for Jennifer. She wanted to beat them so bad.

But if your plan works, you'll definitely beat the Coyotes—and you'll be the hero, not Jennifer, she reminded herself.

The stands began to fill with parents and students from both schools. Tania suddenly felt nervous about using the marble. Would it work with so many people around?

There was only one way to find out. Tania had to be more careful this time, she knew. She waited until the third inning, when the Spiders had a 3-1 lead over the Coyotes, before she used the marble for the first time.

One of the Coyotes hit an easy pop up to the infield. Jennifer ran to catch it—an easy out that would have ended the inning.

Tania held her breath and dropped the marble. It was amazing. The players froze in mid-action, and even the people in the stands had stopped moving, their hands stopped in mid-clap, hot dogs lifted halfway to their mouths.

But she didn't have long. Tania ran to the ball and moved it slightly out of Jennifer's path. Then she ran back to second base.

She counted ten seconds before the scene unfroze again, and Jennifer missed the ball. The Coyote runner made it safely to first base, and the Coyotes scored another run.

Jennifer looked really flustered. Tania could tell her confidence was shaken. In fact, for the rest of the game, Tania only had to use the marble once more to make Jennifer goof up. Jennifer did a pretty good job of goofing up on her own the rest of the time. She walked four batters in the fifth inning. Finally, Coach Merker put Tania on the pitching mound.

This was what Tania had been waiting for. She pitched her heart out, striking out a couple of batters each inning. The fans loved it, and Tania heard some of them chant her name.

It's just like it was before Jennifer came, Tania remembered. *I wish things had never changed.*

Finally, in the ninth inning, the score was Spiders 7, Coyotes 6. Thanks to an unexpected line drive from one of the Coyotes, the bases were loaded with two outs.

Tania cradled the marble in her palm. She threw the ball, watching and waiting. It looked like a . . .

"Strike!" the umpire called out.

Tania let out a breath. So far so good. She

pitched again . . .

"Strike!" called the umpire again.

The crowd cheered. Tania smiled and waved. Then she pitched . . .

But the batter had her eye on the ball, and it looked like she was going to make contact this time. Tania dropped the marble, moved the ball, and made it back to the pitcher's mound just in time to hear . . .

"Strike three!"

The Spiders fans went wild. Tania's teammates picked her up and hoisted her in the air.

"Good job, Tania," Coach Merker exclaimed. "You saved the game."

Tania felt like she was on top of the world—until she saw Lincoln's face. Her friend stood behind home plate, sadly shaking his head. For a split second, Tania felt ashamed.

If Tania keeps using the marble, go to page 136.

If Tania feels guilty and decides to return the marble to the Scream Shop, go to page 94.

But Tania really wanted to try out the marble.

"This is too good to pass up," she said. "If that gargoyle shows up, I'll just freeze him again."

Lincoln walked Tania to the front door. "This is the weirdest thing I've ever heard. Just promise you won't freeze me, okay? That sounds really creepy."

"Don't worry," Tania said. "I'm not going to use it on you. But I have a pretty good idea what I'm going to do with it."

Lincoln groaned. "Oh, no. Not Jennifer! She's really nice, Tania. I don't know why you hate her so much."

Tania suddenly felt angry. She should have guessed that Lincoln would stand up for Jennifer again.

"It's none of your business," Tania snapped. Without saying good-bye, she turned and headed back home.

Tania was glad to find that the gargoyle had gone, and Sunny the goldfish was swimming happily in his bowl. "So, the freezing is only temporary," Tania said out loud, holding the marble between her fingers. "I wonder how long it lasts?"

She'd have to experiment. And she knew exactly when to do it.

Lincoln had been right. She planned to use the marble to mess with Jennifer Delgado. Tomorrow was Saturday, and softball practice was at 11 a.m. It would be the perfect place.

She lay awake for hours, trying to come up with a plan. By the time practice rolled around, Tania was ready.

When Tania got to the practice field, it was swarming with sixth-grade girls in red caps and red T-shirts emblazoned with a black spider, their team mascot. Tania glanced around and spotted Jennifer running around the bases, her long, brown hair streaming out behind her cap. She always ran a few laps to warm up before practice. Coach Merker ate it up.

"That's the spirit, Jennifer," she always said. "I wish all of our players were as dedicated as you."

Actually, Tania knew that running laps wasn't a bad idea, but she wouldn't do it simply because Jennifer did. She did some stretches instead, checking every minute to make sure the marble was still in her front pocket. Then Coach Merker blew her whistle.

The girls took their positions on the field.

"All right, let's take turns batting," Coach Merker called out. "Usual lineup."

Jennifer took her place on the pitcher's mound, and Tania took her spot at second base.

Beth Ivanich batted first. Jennifer lobbed a fastball at her, and Beth hit it, knocking a ground ball aimed straight for the pitcher's mound.

Tania took a deep breath. This is what she had been waiting for. She waited until the ball was inches from Jennifer's glove . . .

And then she dropped the marble.

It was amazing. Everyone had frozen. Both of Beth's feet were off the ground, stopped in time as she headed for first base. Jennifer's face was screwed up in a look of concentration, her eye firmly on the ball.

Tania didn't know how much time she had, so she ran. She picked up the softball and moved it a foot to the right. Then she ran back to second base and waited.

She didn't have to wait long. About ten seconds later, everyone unfroze. And, instead of catching the easy grounder, Jennifer's face registered shock as the ball whizzed right by her. Alice Khan, the infielder, caught the ball instead.

"Look alive, Delgado!" Coach Merker yelled.

Tania grinned. She couldn't believe it! Her plan had worked perfectly. She quietly picked up the marble and returned it to her pocket.

For the rest of practice, Tania used the marble whenever she could. When Jennifer was at bat, she moved the ball out of the way so she struck out every time. She even messed with Jennifer's pitches so that she went a whole inning throwing foul balls.

Tania felt great when practice was over. But her mood swiftly deflated.

"Everyone has a bad day once in a while," Coach Merker was saying to Jennifer. "Don't worry about it. I still want you to start Monday's big game."

Tania stormed off the field, fuming. It wasn't fair! She had played much better than Jennifer today, and still nobody noticed. It was like Jennifer could do nothing wrong.

Tania stormed right into Lincoln, who looked angry himself.

"I watched the last two innings," Lincoln said. "Jennifer played really lousy. Did you have something to do with that?"

Lincoln's attitude was starting to bug her.

"Like I said yesterday, it's none of your business," Tania snapped.

Lincoln looked more worried than angry now. "Listen, Tania, I'm afraid for you. Why don't you just give the marble to your grandfather, like you planned?"

Lincoln's words hit home. She had bought the marble for Grandpa Martin in the first place. Using the marble hadn't helped make things better. Maybe Lincoln was right.

Then again, said a little voice in her head, *imagine what you could do at the big game on Monday. Jennifer would be embarrassed in front of everybody . . .*

If Tania uses the marble at the big game, go to page 108.

If Tania gives the marble to her grandfather, go to page 106.

Continued from page 85

"I'm left-handed," Tania said. "So let's try the left. If we don't see anything, we can always come back."

Kragg nodded, and the two headed left. Tania noticed that they were walking upstream. The water trickled past them, heading in the opposite direction.

From time to time, Tania flashed her light into the dark water. The shiny, black water reflected Tania's face, like some kind of a mirror.

The sound of slowly trickling water was all Tania could hear as she and Kragg made their way down the passage. They walked for a while. Tania shone the light ahead, but couldn't make out anything new.

Another ten minutes passed, and Tania thought about asking Kragg if they should turn back. But before she could get out the words, she heard a splash in the water.

"What's that?" Tania asked. She spun around, aiming her light at the stream.

The surface of the water began to churn. Tania and Kragg stood still, watching. Was this some kind of sign? Some kind of clue to the chamber?

Then suddenly, without warning, a mass of slimy tentacles exploded from the stream. They flailed, grasping at Tania and Kragg.

"Run!" Tania yelled. They charged ahead, but there was only so much room between the stream and the passage wall. The tentacles disappeared under the water, but emerged again farther upstream. Apparently, the creature could swim faster than they could run.

"Faster!" Tania yelled.

Tania's feet pounded on the floor of the passageway. She ran like she had hit a fly ball and was trying to make it all the way home.

And then the ground gave way.

Tania's stomach dropped as she fell . . . and fell. Then she hit the ground with a thud. A huge crashing sound told her that Kragg had fallen, too.

Tania lay still for a moment. Her body hurt all over, but it didn't feel like anything had broken. She had broken her arm during soccer practice once, and that had hurt a lot more than this.

Tania slowly sat up. She reached for the flashlight, which had fallen. Then she shone it around.

She and Kragg had fallen into some kind of deep pit.

"That was not fun," Tania said, standing up. "Are you okay?"

"I am fine," Kragg said.

"Then let's use those wings of yours and fly

out of here," she said. "Mind if I hop on?"

Kragg nodded. He took a step toward Tania. Then he stopped.

"Something is not right," he said. "I cannot move my legs."

"What do you mean?" Tania asked.

"I am turning into my statue form," he said. "But that is not right. It only happens when I am in the sunlight. Unless . . . "

"Unless what?" Tania asked.

"Unless the Dark One has succeeded," Kragg said. "It has stolen our life force."

"No!" Tania cried. She rushed to Kragg's side, but she could see that he was right. His body had frozen in position.

"I . . . am . . . sorry . . . " Kragg said slowly, forcing every word. Then his mouth froze in place.

"Kragg! Kragg!" Tania tried to shake the gargoyle, but he would not budge.

She aimed the flashlight around the pit, looking for a way out. The walls were smooth and slippery—too smooth for rock climbing. Even if she stood on Kragg's back, she couldn't reach the top of the pit.

She was trapped. The Dark One had won.

THE END

Continued from page 70

"Well, I don't care what you think," Tania said testily. She wasn't usually so bossy around Lincoln, but for some reason she felt anxious. "I want to go now!"

"All right! All right!" Lincoln gave in. "Can we just eat lunch first? I'm starving."

Tania groaned, but she had to admit that she felt hungry, too.

"Fine," Tania said. "Let's make it quick."

Tania took the white marble from Lincoln and stashed it safely in her pocket with the black one. They ate lunch at Lincoln's house, and took even longer than expected when Lincoln had to help his little brother fix his bike. Finally, they headed off.

Lincoln kept telling Tania he knew where this round park was. He led the way from his neighborhood to downtown Bleaktown. They rode for about a half hour until they came to an abandoned warehouse. Lincoln hopped off his bike, scratching his head.

"I'm sure this was the way," he said.

"Lincoln, let me see the directions," Tania said annoyingly.

"Uh, I forgot them." Lincoln blushed.

"I'll find it!" Lincoln snapped. Tania followed

him again, into a neighborhood that she had never seen before. Large, fancy houses lined the streets.

"This is near where my aunt lives!" Lincoln said excitedly. "I recognize it now. We're almost there."

"We'd better be," Tania said. The sun was starting to sink into the sky. If that legend was true, the gargoyles might be awake soon. She wasn't sure if she wanted to be around when that happened.

But Lincoln was right this time. They turned a corner and found themselves facing a large, round park that was surrounded by an ivy-covered, stone wall. *It is much nicer than Bleaktown Park,* Tania decided, as they stepped inside. Red and purple flowers grew around marble benches. Old-fashioned street lamps flanked the benches; their lamps had just turned on in the dim light of dusk. A stream ran around the entire circle, passable by a covered bridge.

And in the very center, atop a tall pedestal, sat a gargoyle.

Tania ran across the bridge to get a closer look. Just as she thought, the gargoyle had two silver marbles for eyes. Without waiting, Tania started to climb up.

"Tania!" Lincoln called up.

"I've almost got it," Tania snapped back. She

had fished out her penknife and was prying around the glowing silver marble.

"Tania!" Lincoln called again. "The sun is down now! Look!"

Tania looked up at the dusky blue sky. The sun had indeed gone down. But she was so close to being done . . .

"WHO DARES TO DISTURB MY REST?" a voice screamed.

Tania almost fell off the pedestal. The gargoyle had risen from his crouched position. His silver eyes stared at Tania angrily.

"I-I just wanted—" Tania stammered.

"Tania! Get down!"

Lincoln's voice snapped Tania out of her fear. She jumped down off the pedestal. The gargoyle opened his gray, leathery wings and swooped down after her.

"YOU SHALL PAY!" he growled.

Tania hopped on her bike and hurriedly pedaled out of the park, with Lincoln following quickly behind her. After what seemed like hours, they finally reached Tania's driveway.

Tania jumped off her bike and said quietly, "I guess that wasn't such a good idea, after all."

Lincoln slowly nodded in agreement.

THE END

Continued from page 82

Elias sounded like he meant business. Probably because Lincoln was afraid of Elias more than the birds, he ran back to the gargoyle.

"Do not move," Elias warned. He began to chant again.

Lincoln tried to figure out what the gargoyle was saying, but he couldn't. It sounded like Elias was talking in some kind of strange language.

Lincoln almost asked Elias what he was doing, but decided against it. Instead, he stood silently by the gargoyle's side, watching as the birds got closer and closer.

It didn't look like the birds understood Elias's language, either. They screeched and cawed as they dove in for the attack. The sound of their beating wings made the ground shake underneath them.

Lincoln couldn't watch anymore. He closed his eyes and muttered a prayer under his breath.

Then, suddenly, everything went quiet. Lincoln cautiously opened his eyes.

The birds were silently falling from the sky, changing shape as they descended. Lincoln couldn't believe what he was seeing. By the time each bird hit the ground, it had completely transformed into a small, black flower. Within seconds, the mountainside was covered with them.

Elias stopped chanting. He studied the flowers and nodded.

"Let's go," he said to Lincoln.

"Wait a second!" Lincoln cried. "What happened here? What did you do?"

The gargoyle sighed. "I used an ancient charm against evil. The birds that attacked us began life as flowers. The Dark One transformed them for its own evil purposes. The chant I spoke turned the birds back to their true form."

"It's a good thing their original form was flowers, and not fire-breathing dragons or something," Lincoln remarked. "At least flowers can't hurt us."

Elias shook his head. "I don't know how you humans have survived for so long. Those flowers are highly poisonous. To your kind, anyway. Now, let's go."

Lincoln blushed and followed Elias up the mountain.

I guess I must seem like some stupid kid to Elias, Lincoln thought. *He's been around forever, fighting evil and stuff. He must think I'm useless.*

They walked for another fifteen minutes, and Lincoln had the urge to speak again. He couldn't help himself. His mom said he liked talking better than breathing.

"So, the Dark One must be pretty powerful,

huh?" Lincoln asked.

"Of course," Elias replied.

"Maybe you should tell me something about it," Lincoln said. "That way I'll know how to fight it. I can help."

Elias turned and looked at Lincoln, who noticed for the first time that the gargoyle had stones for eyes like Kragg. But Elias's eyes were gold.

"Tell me, human," Elias said. "Have you ever fought a nightmare? A terror that crawls into your brain, preying on your innermost fears? Or, do you wake up screaming in terror, searching for light?"

It took a minute for the gargoyle's words to sink in. If the Dark One was like a nightmare, Lincoln figured Elias was right. He wouldn't even know how to fight it. Lincoln didn't know what to say.

Elias snorted again—a sound Lincoln was starting to get used to.

"I thought as much," Elias said. "Continue to do as I say. I will keep you safe. I need you."

Lincoln frowned and followed the gargoyle. He tried not to think about what might happen when they got to the chamber. He hoped he wouldn't let Elias down.

Then, Elias's ears perked up. The gargoyle

stopped. Lincoln listened.

A loud, humming sound was coming toward them. Lincoln struggled to see in the darkness. But Elias already knew.

"Bees," Elias said. "More messengers from the Dark One."

Elias began the chant again. The swarm of bees came closer and closer.

"There must be a million of them," Lincoln whispered. He imagined what it would feel like to be stung by them and shuddered.

Elias kept chanting. The bees kept coming. And coming.

"The chant is not working," Elias said. "The Dark One must have conjured the bees some other way. We must run."

Lincoln looked around. A clump of pine trees rose up on the left. On the right, he could make out a shelter of overhanging rock.

"Which way?" Lincoln asked.

If Lincoln and Elias run to the trees, go to page 57.
If Lincoln and Elias run to the rock, go to page 96.

"Let's check out the library," Tania said. "That's a better idea."

They rode back toward Main Street and turned down Bookman Drive, a dead end. The Bleaktown Library rose up majestically at the end of the block. The old, stone building had two floors and a massive front door. A more modern-looking extension made of brick branched out from the building's left side.

The library was closed on Sunday, so Tania and Lincoln could snoop around outside without being noticed. They walked around the extension of the library, which housed the children's wing, looking up as they went. There was nothing on the back wall, either.

Finally, they turned the corner, and spotted the gargoyle on the right side of the building. It was nestled on a half-moon-shaped ledge, just like the one on the church. Luckily, the stone wall had just as many nooks and crevices, too, so Tania was able to climb up as she had done before.

Like the others, this gargoyle had unique features. Its long, pointed nose looked like a bird's beak, and its glittering gold eyes were set into two spiral-shaped sockets. The gold marble on the left had the familiar glow, so Tania pried it out with her penknife. Then she carefully climbed back down.

"So," Tania said. "We've got all four. Let's see what kind of powers these marbles have!"

Tania and Lincoln found a secluded spot in the back of the library, underneath a tall tree. They sat cross-legged on the grass, facing each other. Tania arranged the four marbles in a circle between them.

The marbles began to glow more brightly than they had done before. Once again, they rose up from the ground, swirling and twirling in the air. But something was different this time.

A gray mist formed around the marbles as they swirled above. Tania and Lincoln watched, open-mouthed, as the mist took shape before their eyes.

Soon, the ghostly form of a man stood between them. His body was completely made of mist, but they could clearly make out his clothes and features. He was a short man, with two beady eyes set in a round face and a head topped with stringy, balding hair. He wore an old-fashioned-looking vest over a button-down shirt, and his pants were tucked into a pair of black boots with buckles.

Tania slowly inched her way toward Lincoln's side. Lincoln grabbed her hand and squeezed it.

The ghostly man eyed them suspiciously.

"Who are you strange folk?" he asked. "Are you sorcerers?"

Tania shook her head. "N-N-No," she stammered, talking quickly out of nervousness. "We read about the four marbles in a book, and we were curious, so we found the gargoyles and took the stones and then they started to twirl—"

The man grinned. "Ah, my fine grotesques. So, you have discovered their secret?"

"What's a grow-tesk?" Lincoln asked. Tania knew he couldn't keep silent for long.

"Grotesques are my statues, my lovely deformed creatures," he said. "I made them, you see. I am—or was—one of the greatest stone carvers who ever lived. You must have heard of me. I am Mason Talbot." He beamed, waiting for them to praise him.

"Uh, sure," Tania fibbed. "So, they can really come to life at night?"

The stone carver nodded. "They are my greatest creations," he said.

"You know, I was wondering," Tania said, feeling a little braver. "The book said that the stones are really powerful when you keep them together. So why did you split them up?"

Talbot's face darkened. "It was a necessity. I used the power of the marbles against my enemies. I was able to turn anyone I desired into stone. But then I was found out. I scattered the marbles among my precious gargoyles. I knew they would keep them safe for me until my return."

He beamed at Tania and Lincoln. "I am grateful to you for bringing me back. With your help, I will seek revenge on my enemies! I will turn them all to stone, sparing no one."

Tania and Lincoln exchanged glances. This stone-carver guy was downright evil.

"Didn't you live a long time ago?" Tania asked him. "All of your enemies must be dead by now."

"Then I will destroy their descendants!" Talbot said, his eyes flashing.

Tania took a step back. "That sounds great," she said. "Let me confer with my . . . fellow sorcerer here."

Tania whispered in Lincoln's ear. "We've got to get rid of this guy," she said. "I'm thinking we could attack him."

"He's made of mist," Lincoln replied. "Let's smash the marbles. I bet he'll disappear."

"Smash the marbles? No way," Tania said. "Then we'll never get to find out all the things they can do."

"I think we should go after Talbot," Tania said confidently. "There are two of us—we can do it. Then we'll be able to keep the marbles for ourselves."

"Well, we have to do something," Lincoln hissed. "And we have to decide now!"

Tania nodded. It was now or never.

If Tania and Lincoln decide to destroy the marbles, go to page 47.

If Tania and Lincoln decide to attack Talbot instead, go to page 86.

Continued from page 46

Don't listen to it, Tania told herself. *It's a trick. You need to help Kragg.*

But she could feel the Dark One pulling at her—almost like it had curled up inside her brain like a snake. And she liked what she heard.

"Tania! Are you all right?" Kragg called out.

The sound of Kragg's voice jarred the hold that the Dark One had on her. For a split second, Tania felt free. She used that time to call out to Kragg.

"It's the Dark One!" she yelled. "It's like, in my brain or something."

"You must shut it out!" Kragg said urgently. "Leave the chalice if you must. But do not let the Dark One take hold!"

"I'm not giving up now!" Tania yelled back. She grabbed the chalice. Immediately, she heard the voice of the Dark One again.

"Drink it, Tania," it hissed. "Drink it, and the power of the gargoyles shall be yours."

Without realizing, Tania found herself raising the cup to her lips. The Dark One's words sounded so tempting. All she had to do was drink . . .

"Tania!" Kragg's voice snapped her out of it again.

"Sorry," Tania said. She lowered the chalice

and dashed toward the chamber door.

Kragg took the chalice out of her hand as soon as she came through.

"You did it, Tania," he said. "Your strength has served you well."

"Perhaps not well enough," a voice eerily spoke. Around them, a black mist had begun to form. The mist became more solid as it circled around them.

"You may have resisted me in the chamber," the Dark One said, "but here my power is strong."

The Dark One began to take form. To her horror, Tania watched it turn into a giant, black snake. The snake curled around Tania and Kragg, trapping them in its coils. The head of the snake formed last. It slowly leaned in toward them. Tania found herself frozen in fear, staring help-lessly into its yellow eyes.

"The chalice shall be mine," hissed the Dark One.

"You shall not win!" Kragg cried, his black eyes gleaming.

"Oh, but I shall," said the snake. "You are not powerful enough to stop me, Kragg."

"But we are!" Tania heard other voices call out.

A spark of hope jolted through Tania. Over

the coils of the snake, she could see the beaked face of Elias and the other gargoyles. Lincoln stood with them.

The eyes of the gargoyles began to gleam. Beams of white light shot from their eyes, zapping the Dark One.

"This is not the end!" the Dark One hissed. Then the snake vanished into thin air.

"Lincoln!" Tania ran to her friend. "How did you find us?"

"The gargoyles tore through the fallen rocks," he said. "Man, they are strong. Then we followed the map."

Elias pushed past them both to get to Kragg. "Is the chalice safe?" he asked.

"Yes," Kragg said. "Thanks to Tania."

Elias snorted, but he looked happy. "You know what we must do," he said.

Kragg nodded. "It is time."

Then Kragg lifted the chalice to his lips and took a sip.

"Hey!" Tania cried. "I thought it was bad to drink that stuff."

"Foolish girl," Elias said. "This life force belongs to us. It will make us stronger. Once we all drink from it, we will be able to move in day-light as well as night."

Tania thought about this. "So why didn't the

stone carver let you drink it before?"

Kragg passed the chalice to Elias. "Our creators were afraid to give us too much power. They feared we would join the Dark One, and they wanted a way to control us. But we have passed the test of time. We need this power now if we are to succeed."

The rest of the gargoyles drank from the chalice. Then Kragg led the way back up the passage.

"This was pretty amazing," Lincoln told Tania. "I can't believe we won!"

"Yeah," Tania agreed. It felt even better than winning a softball game. But something still bothered her.

What if she had never found that marble in Sebastian Cream's shop? Then none of this would have happened. It seemed too weird to just be a coincidence.

There was one way to find out. Tomorrow, she would ask Sebastian Cream about it. She just hoped he had some answers.

Go to page 142.

Then Tania's teammates started chanting her name again, and she forgot all about feeling ashamed. On the bus ride home, she sat in the front while the rest of the girls fussed over her, asking her about her big strikeout. Jennifer sulked in the backseat.

This is the way it should be, Tania reasoned. *It's the way it was before Jennifer came.* Tania was just using the marble to make things right again. What was wrong with that?

When she got home, she found Lincoln waiting on her front steps.

"Great game, huh?" Tania asked.

Lincoln frowned. "You should give back that marble, Tania," he said. "It's not right. It's not fair to Jennifer."

"Not fair to Jennifer?" Tania snapped. "Was it fair that Coach Merker gave her my batting slot and my position when I'm just as good as she is? So don't talk to me about fair."

Tania stomped into the house.

Lincoln didn't talk to her the next day at school, but Tania didn't care. She had enough attention from everyone else. In gym class, Coach Merker told Tania she'd be pitching at the Spiders' next game.

"I won't let you down," Tania promised. *I'll just use my marble,* she added silently to herself.

Two days later, Tania got suited up for a game against the Wombats, the team from August Bleaker Elementary School across town. Tania had spent the last forty-eight hours coming up with a strategy for this game. She didn't have to worry so much about making Jennifer look bad anymore. She just had to make sure that she looked good. *Really* good.

Since the Wombats were batting first, Tania would be throwing the first pitch. She had decided to start off the game by striking out the pitcher, just to keep her reputation going.

Tania Robbins, the Strikeout Queen. She liked the sound of that.

The Wombats' first batter walked to the plate. Tania threw her first ball straight down the line. A perfect strike.

Tania's teammates cheered. She was on a roll. Tania threw the next ball, and watched as it veered to the left, a sure foul ball. Tania frowned. That was no way to start out. She threw the marble to the ground.

Tania started to run to home plate to move the ball, but realized that she couldn't seem to move. She watched as the catcher caught the ball, heard the umpire cry, "Ball one!", but she couldn't seem to move a muscle.

The other players noticed it, too. Tania heard a murmur go up from the crowd as the umpire blew his whistle. Her teammates crowded around her.

"Are you okay, Tania?" Coach Merker asked.

Tania tried to answer, but she couldn't move her mouth. Something was terribly, horribly wrong.

This time, she was frozen!

Don't panic, she told herself. *It only lasts for a little while. You'll be back to normal soon.*

Tania counted to ten in her head . . . then twenty . . . then thirty. Nothing. She heard the siren of an ambulance in the distance and watched her teammates whisper to one another, throwing her curious glances.

Lincoln pushed through the crowd. He walked up to Tania, a sad look on his face.

"I knew something like this would happen," he said. "I wish you had taken that stupid marble back!"

THE END

Continued from page 99

Lincoln looked at Tania holding the chalice. She looked like some kind of crazed zombie. Lincoln decided that trying to grab the chalice from her was a bad idea. He wasn't exactly a physical guy—but he was great at talking.

"You are so right, Tania!" Lincoln said. "Who cares about these stupid gargoyles? They're just a bunch of human-hating freaks."

He heard Elias growl behind him. But Tania looked interested. She lowered the chalice.

"I'll drink the life force with you," he said. "We'll rule the world together. It'll be awesome."

Lincoln held out his hand, but Tania eyed him suspiciously.

"I want to go first," she said.

Lincoln had been expecting this.

"Fine," he said casually. "I just hope that alchemist guy didn't put anything weird in there."

"What do you mean?" Tania asked.

Lincoln shrugged. "I don't know. I guess they could have put something in it to keep people from drinking it. Like, maybe if you're not a gargoyle and you drink it, you'll explode or something. But I'm probably being silly. You should go first."

Tania thrust the chalice into Lincoln's hands.

"No, you go first," she said.

Lincoln tried not to smile. His trick had worked. He lifted the chalice to his lips, and pretended to take a sip . . .

And then he ran.

"Let's go!" he hissed to Elias.

Lincoln heard Tania let out a painful cry. Elias took the chalice from Lincoln, then grabbed him and flew out of the cavern, back onto the mountainside.

A few minutes later, Tania emerged from the hole. She looked back to normal.

"You did it, Lincoln!" Tania said excitedly. "When you took the chalice, the Dark One took off. You did it!"

"Wow!" exclaimed Lincoln. "I guess I did, huh?"

Beaming, Lincoln looked at Elias. Would the gargoyle give him any credit?

"Not bad, for a human," Elias said. "I am grateful. The chalice is safe now, and I can use its power to rescue my people from the cave-in."

"Kragg is on the other side of the chamber," Tania said. "I'll tell him to head back to the cavern." She disappeared down the hole again.

"So," Lincoln asked, "can I help you rescue the others? Now that I am a hero and all."

Elias sighed. "I suppose it can't hurt," he said.

Lincoln grinned. Elias would never be a big fan of humans.

But it still felt great to win!

THE END

Continued from pages 105, 135

The next day Tania woke up early with anxiety. She barely ate her breakfast. She couldn't wait to go back to Sebastian Cream's shop, but she had no idea what time it opened.

Finally, at nine o'clock, Tania couldn't wait any longer. She hopped on her bike and rode to Wary Lane.

As she pulled up to the shop, she found Sebastian Cream opening the front door with a key. He wore a funny-looking red cap on his head.

"Ah, Tania," he said, smiling at her. "Good morning! Are you here to find another marble?"

"Not exactly," Tania said. "I have a few questions for you."

Mr. Cream's green eyes twinkled. "Well, you are in luck. We are having a sale on answers today. That is, if I have the answers you are looking for. Please, come inside."

Tania followed Mr. Cream into the crowded shop. He walked to the counter and took off his cap.

"So, dear," he said, settling on his stool. "What is your question?"

"It's about the marble I found," she said. "Where did you find it?"

Mr. Cream shrugged. "I have so many objects in my shop. How can I keep track of them all?"

Tania took a deep breath. "But you have to remember about this one. It wasn't a marble at all. It belonged to a gargoyle. And he came looking for it. And—"

Mr. Cream held up his left hand. "You are full of questions today, my dear. But I don't think you need my answers. Things worked out just fine, didn't they?"

Tania nodded.

"Then that's all you need to know," he said firmly. "Now, why don't you run along. I must get ready for business."

Mr. Cream stood up from his stool and ushered Tania out of the store. She found herself on the front step, more confused than before.

Tania turned back to her bike. There was a kid standing next to it, staring into the window. Tania recognized him. It was Matt Carter, a kid from another school. Tania knew him because he was always hanging around softball practice, asking her for pointers.

"Hey, Matt," Tania said. "What's up?"

"Uh, not much," Matt answered distractedly. He was staring intently at something in the window of the junk shop.

Tania looked at Matt strangely, but then just

shrugged and got on her bike.

Maybe Mr. Cream was right.

Everything had turned out fine. That's all she needed to know.

THE END

A Prosperity Classic

THE
GAME
OF
LIFE

A N D

how to play it

FLORENCE SCOVEL
SHINN